Faded Dreams

Live! From Brentwood High

1 ▪ Risky Assignment
2 ▪ Price of Silence
3 ▪ Double Danger
4 ▪ Sarah's Dilemma
5 ▪ Undercover Artists
6 ▪ Faded Dreams

9607

Faded Dreams

JUDY BAER

BETHANY HOUSE PUBLISHERS
MINNEAPOLIS, MINNESOTA 55438

Cover illustration by Joe Nordstrom

Library of Congress Catalog Card Number 96–25286

ISBN 1–55661–391–1

Published by Bethany House Publishers
A Ministry of Bethany Fellowship, Inc.
11300 Hampshire Avenue South
Minneapolis, Minnesota 55438

Printed in the United States of America.

For Carolyn,

who is taking the journey with me.

JUDY BAER received a B.A. in English and Education from Concordia College in Moorhead, Minnesota. She has had over thirty novels published and is a member of the National Romance Writers of America, the Society of Children's Book Writers, and the National Federation of Press Women.

Two of her novels, *Adrienne* and *Paige*, have been prizewinning bestsellers in the Bethany House SPRINGFLOWER SERIES (for girls 12–15). Both books have been awarded first place for juvenile fiction in the National Federation of Press Women's communications contest.

LIVE
FROM BRENTWOOD HIGH

Julie Osborn entered the media room waving a fistful of photos. "You have to see these. They are so cute!"

Jake Sanders and Shane Donahue turned their heads toward Julie, but Darby Ellison, Molly Ashton, and Kate Akima, who were scanning copy for the next newscast, didn't even look up. Josh Willis and Sarah Riley were deep in conversation across the room and hadn't noticed Julie's arrival.

"Look at this baby." Julie thrust the photos in front of Jake and Shane.

Andrew Tremaine sauntered over, glanced at the pictures, and yawned. "So? It's only a baby. The way you were talking, I thought maybe you had pictures of a new car or something."

Julie's lip curled. "A *car*? Why would I get so excited about a car?"

"It's more interesting than a baby," Shane commented. "Don't you think so, Jake?"

"Depends. Now if it were *my* car, then I'd definitely be interested."

"Hey! You'd be excited if it were your baby, too, wouldn't you?" Shane and Andrew guffawed but sobered quickly when Julie glared at them.

"It's not *your* baby, is it?" Andrew gulped.

"Of course not! Did you exchange your brains for your breakfast this morning? It's my cousin's baby. She had her last week. Isn't she the most darling thing you've ever seen? She looks just like her daddy except for her nose. She definitely has her mother's nose. . . ."

"Poor mother," Izzy Mooney commented as he entered from editing bay B. "She lost her nose? Hope she doesn't wear glasses. They'd be really hard to keep on her face. Of course, maybe she could rig up some sort of strap to ride on her ears and keep them tight to her head. . . ."

"Stop it! All of you!"

Izzy blinked. His dandelion-like fluff of buzz-cut hair stood on end. He straightened huge shoulders under his wrinkled flannel shirt and stared at Julie. Shane and Andrew snapped to attention. The girls looked up from their reading. Josh and Sarah glanced at the flustered group in confusion.

"What'd we do?"

"Nobody's paying attention except you, Isador, and you're making fun. My cousin just had her baby. This is very important to me. I'm trying to tell you something special about my life and no one will listen!"

"Julie, it's just a baby. People have them all the

time," Andrew pointed out. "Besides, what are we supposed to do about it?"

"I can't believe you people!" She thrust the photos under Andrew's nose. "Isn't that child adorable?"

Now everyone had gathered around Julie and her pictures, curious to see what was so exceptional about this child.

"She's very sweet," Sarah offered from her wheelchair. "I can see why you're excited."

"At least *one* person appreciates little Julie Marie besides me."

"The baby is *named* after you?" Andrew whistled. "Those parents must be *nuts*!"

Julie didn't take the bait. Instead, she stared lovingly at the photos. "I think my cousin is so lucky to have her."

"Lucky? No way!" Izzy grimaced. " 'Lucky' isn't the way I'd describe having a baby." Everyone knew he was remembering his experience with a computerized doll for his Home Living class. He'd nearly driven them insane with his overprotectiveness, his requests for baby-sitters, and complaints about being tied down.

"That wasn't a real baby you were taking care of," Julie pointed out. "It was a doll and an assignment."

"That's right. And it was awful. I couldn't go anywhere or do anything unless that dumb doll was accounted for. I was tired of having a baby when I was done with the assignment—and my baby wasn't even *real*!"

"Just think what it would have been like if it had been a live baby and there was no way you could give it back!" Molly speculated.

Izzy shuddered so that his entire body quivered—an awesome sight in one so large. "No thanks."

"I don't agree," Julie said. "I think it would be wonderful to have a baby of your own."

"Someday," Darby said. "But not now."

Molly gave a sharp little intake of air. Every head turned toward her. "I know I shouldn't be gossiping. . . ."

" . . . but you will anyway," Andrew added.

"I heard that one of the senior girls is expecting a baby. It's due right after graduation."

"Really? Will she graduate with her class?" Kate questioned, interested in technical details.

"Is she getting married?" Darby asked.

"Bummer," Shane said with a shrug. Andrew and Jake nodded.

"Is that all you guys can say?" Kate asked disgustedly. "You act as if you aren't even interested."

"It's not exactly our business," Jake pointed out. "Or ours to do anything about either."

"But don't you think about what it would be like if it *did* involve you?"

"I hope we're too smart for that," Shane said pointedly. "It's stupid to mess around and a good way to wreck your entire life."

"I think it would be really scary," Molly said sympathetically. Everyone could tell she was imagining herself in the shoes of that senior girl. "You couldn't be a kid anymore because you'd *have* a kid of your own."

"It would be very sad," Sarah said softly. As a Christian, Sarah always had an interesting take on what the others were discussing. Her green eyes grew moist. "That poor girl."

"What makes you think it's sad?" Kate asked. "Difficult, yes. Embarrassing, maybe. But sad?"

"I believe sex should be saved for marriage," Sarah said bluntly. They'd been together through a lot since they'd joined the *Live! From Brentwood High* media team. She could be as honest and forthright with these people as with anyone. "Virginity should be the best and most wonderful gift you can give your husband or wife."

"Oh, Sarah, you sound so old-fashioned sometimes!" Julie exclaimed.

Before Sarah could respond, Izzy chimed in. "I agree with Sarah. It isn't right to bring a child into the world without two parents to love it. Maybe my reasons aren't as biblical as Sarah's, but they're good ones too. Babies are too hard to raise with only one parent."

"Your only experience was with a *doll*, Isador. Besides, maybe you just aren't very 'maternal,' " Kate said.

"I'm plenty 'maternal,' " Izzy insisted. "I practically raised my twin sisters—with my parents' and grandmother's help, of course, but I'm not crazy." He crossed his beefy arms over his chest and frowned. "It's just too hard for teenagers to have children. My experience proves that, no matter what the rest of you say!"

"You can't make a decision for everyone," Julie pointed out, a defensive note creeping into her voice. "Just because *you* couldn't do it doesn't mean that no one can. Some people are very mature." The way she said "mature" told everyone that she believed Izzy didn't have that particular quality.

"Nobody is mature as a senior in high school," Izzy protested. "Ask anybody's parents!"

Jake and Josh howled with laughter, but Julie was determined to continue the conversation in a more serious vein.

"You boys certainly aren't mature enough to raise a child," she grumbled. "I'm not sure you're old enough to have a driver's license yet."

"Hey!" Izzy protested.

Julie continued. "If I had a baby while I was in high school, I know I'd want to keep it and raise it myself. I'd do a good job too!"

"Maybe you would," Darby said softly, "but that doesn't mean you *should*."

"I don't get it." Julie looked puzzled.

"Having a baby before you graduate or get married is really taking the steps of your life out of order."

"Darby's right there," Molly agreed. "Lots of girls who get pregnant in high school decide to give their babies up for adoption."

"What do you think, Sarah?" Julie turned to the girl in the wheelchair.

Sarah had been listening intently, a serious expression on her face. "I don't suppose I need to say that the best option is to not get into that predicament in the first place."

"We all know that," Kate said impatiently. "Tell us what you really think."

"Adoption is better than abortion. Chastity until marriage is the best of all."

"Chastity? What kind of old-fashioned word is that?" Kate sneered.

"Virginity, then. Purity. Call it what you like. You know what I mean."

The boys were listening intently but not contributing to the conversation. Josh and Andrew looked vaguely embarrassed.

"But what if you *do* get pregnant?" Julie persisted. "Not everyone is wise enough to make the right choices. If a girl finds out she's pregnant, doesn't believe in abortion, and has a boyfriend who doesn't want to marry her—then what?"

At that moment, Ms. Wright cleared her throat. She'd been sitting quietly at her desk going over some papers. Today the *Live! From Brentwood High* advisor wore her hair in a cascade of curls that tumbled down the back of her head. She wore a thick fisherman-knit sweater over a one-piece denim jumper and heavy metallic bracelets on each arm.

"If I might get a word in edgewise . . ."

Gary Richmond, *Live's* professional photographer and part-time instructor, chuckled from his vantage point in a saggy, overstuffed chair nearby. Neither Gary nor Rosie Wright jumped into conversations lightly, so it was obvious that Ms. Wright must have a strong opinion on the topic they were discussing. "Now you've done it," Gary drawled. "You've got Ms. Wright's interest. You know what that means."

They all certainly did. Controversial topics were always bantered about in "Chaos Central," the nickname of Brentwood High's media room and center for the student-run cable television show and class. When Ms. Wright focused on something that was discussed, it usually turned into research and an interviewing and filming assignment for someone.

With her usual dramatic flair, Ms. Wright lifted her briefcase to the top of her desk and opened it. From its depths, she withdrew a thin pamphlet.

"I'm almost afraid to ask," Jake murmured, "but what's that?"

"A flyer I received in the mail a few days ago," Ms. Wright said. "I tucked it away because I thought it might come in handy one day. I never dreamed I'd want it so soon."

Ever curious, Molly moved closer to the desk. "Haven House," she read. "What's that?"

"It's a private organization run by a group of local churches that provides a transition from teenage life to that of being a full-time mother."

"Who can do that?" Molly wondered aloud. "Don't

you have to do that yourself?"

Ms. Wright smiled. "Good point, but Haven House tries to make things easier for girls in that situation."

"Is it like the alternative school on the other side of Brentwood?" Kate inquired. "I've known girls who switched to that program once they found out they were pregnant."

"Or like those 'homes for unwed mothers' my grandma talked about?" Julie added. "Where girls go to live until their babies are born?"

"Not quite like any of them," Ms. Wright responded. "It's a home where girls can live *after* they give birth until they get their feet on the ground. Not every girl wants to stay in her home community after the baby comes. Some girls are asked to leave their parents' homes. Others have been on their own for a while but can't quite manage with a little one. Haven House provides a place to live, schooling, child-care classes, job counseling, therapy—whatever a girl needs to get herself and her child off to a good start."

"I thought *parents* were supposed to do that!" Darby said, surprised.

"Sometimes that doesn't work out," Ms. Wright said gently. "Maybe the parents don't have the financial means to help . . . or the desire. Haven House provides just that—a haven—for school-aged moms who need help."

Ms. Wright continued. "Haven House helps the girls who go there to answer the hard questions—'What do I need to know to raise a child?' 'How can I adjust to the lifestyle having a child requires?' That sort of thing."

"It's good to know that there are places to find help," Sarah commented. "I wonder how many people know about Haven House?"

Shane snapped his fingers. "Here it comes."

Ms. Wright chuckled. "Need I say it?"

"Why don't you students do a story on Haven House?" Andrew and Jake chimed together, mimicking Ms. Wright's often repeated phrases. "It would be a great story for *Live! From Brentwood High.*"

Ms. Wright turned to Gary, who was smiling. "Do you think they know me too well?"

"You are getting predictable," he commented as he leaned a little farther back in his chair. His eyes twinkled beneath shaggy hair.

"I think it's a wonderful idea," Sarah said enthusiastically. "It's important we do stories that can improve our community. If just one student hears about the help she can get from Haven House and it changes her life and that of her child, well . . . that would be awesome!"

"Great." Ms. Wright picked up her pen and jotted a name in her notebook. "Then you can work on this story." She looked around the room. "Any other volunteers?"

"I'm free," Molly said. "I wrapped up what I was working on yesterday."

"Super." Ms. Wright glanced at the guys. "I'm not going to let you men get by without having a representative on this story, you know. It's not just a woman's issue, or at least it *shouldn't* be."

"Josh will do it," Andrew volunteered.

Josh looked startled. His eyes widened in his dusky face. "I will?"

"Sure. You're perfect. You're soft-spoken, you can act like a gentleman, you're sensitive . . . besides, girls like to talk to you."

"They do?" Josh scratched through his black curls looking more and more puzzled.

"You bet. You aren't obnoxious like me. You'd be ideal for this story."

"Thank you, Andrew, for a very impressive job of attempting to talk yourself out of an assignment!" Ms. Wright laughed. "Under most circumstances, that would be my very *best* reason for putting you on this story, but for once, I agree with you."

"That he's obnoxious?" Julie chimed. "We *all* agree with that!"

"No, that Josh is a very sensitive listener. That's important in this case. Very perceptive of you, Andrew."

Now it was Andrew's turn to look puzzled. He was trying to sort out Julie's slam and Ms. Wright's compliment, given within seconds of each other.

"Will you help Molly and Sarah with this assignment, Josh?"

He paused for a moment, then nodded. The other guys gave audible sighs of relief. Jake slapped Josh on the back. "I'm glad this one is yours."

Josh rolled his eyes. Sarah patted him on the hand. "It will be fine. Don't worry. It's not just a 'girl' story. Those babies have fathers too."

He gave a little groan. "I hope I'm not in over my head!"

"How about the rest of us?" Izzy asked. "What should we be working on?"

Ms. Wright reached into her briefcase again. This time she pulled out a letter, which she handed to Izzy. "Read it aloud, please."

Izzy made a big production of unfolding the single sheet of paper inside the envelope.

" 'Dear Mr. Wentworth, the Chamber of Commerce in Brentwood is currently focusing on our city's youth—their interests and needs—both present and future. We understand that your media class often undertakes investigative projects. Would they be interested in pursuing the topic 'Teens for the Twenty-First Century'? If there is interest, please contact us at . . .' Wow!" Izzy's eyes grew large.

"Any takers?" Ms. Wright asked, already knowing the answer.

"You bet!" Jake said. "But what will we be expected to do?"

"Surveys in the junior high schools and upper-elementary grades. Find out what kids like now—and what they think they'll like in the future."

"Amazing," Jake said thoughtfully.

"What are you talking about?" Molly asked.

"Our new assignments. Quite a contrast, don't you

think? Some of us will be researching teens with their futures spread out before them, ready to be created. Meanwhile Sarah, Molly, and Josh will be talking to girls whose futures are already committed—to a baby, probably to a home and job, to responsibility. It's weird how people so close in age can be living such different lives."

"I never promised you this would be easy," Ms. Wright said. Then her eyes began to twinkle. "But I can promise you that *Live! From Brentwood High* will always be interesting!"

"Darby, hi. It's Sarah."

"What's up?" Darby stretched and yawned. She'd been hunkered over her school books too long and was getting stiff.

"Are you studying?"

"What else? I nearly broke my back carrying textbooks home today."

"Me too. I'm sick of studying," Sarah admitted. "Do you want a break?"

"What do you have in mind?"

"Go to the gym with me. I want to work out."

"I didn't know you went to the gym!"

"You can't tell by looking at me what a good athlete I am?" Sarah asked sarcastically. In her wheel chair, Sarah hardly looked athletic, but with her, looks could be deceiving. "I'll pick you up in my van. Give me twenty minutes to get there."

The receiver clicked before Darby had a chance to say goodbye. That meant she'd better hurry. Sarah meant business.

Sarah was obviously well known at the gym. Several staff members greeted her as did a number of the gym patrons.

"Brought a friend tonight, I see," said the man at the desk. "What happened to the big guy with the fuzzy hair?"

"Oh, he wimped out on me," Sarah said with a laugh. "You know those big guys—all talk, no show."

"*Izzy* lifted weights with you?" Darby marveled. "And wimped out?"

"He just couldn't lift as much as he thought he should," Sarah said with a laugh. "It was hard on his ego. I have a hunch that he'll be back—after he does a little private working out first."

"You showed him up, huh?" Darby smiled at the thought.

"Me? I'm in a wheelchair, remember? I couldn't do that!" Sarah led Darby toward the ladies' locker room, a pale gray and lavender room with banks of lockers, showers, and sinks. There was a large hot tub in the far corner.

"This is great!" Darby said. "Do you come here often?"

"As often as I can," Sarah said as she opened her locker. "I need to stay in shape. Upper-arm strength is vital for me because it keeps me mobile—pushing the wheels on my chair.

"Here, you can put your stuff in my locker when we go into the weight room."

Sarah was already wearing her workout clothes

and had only to pull off her windbreaker. Darby quickly changed into the shorts and T-shirt she had brought.

As Darby dressed, they discussed their new assignment. "When are you going to start working on the school-aged moms program?" she asked.

"Soon. Josh, Molly, and I talked about it today. We're eager to begin—especially me."

"Why do you say that?" Darby did a few stretching exercises to warm up.

"I'm not sure. I just know that I feel a real . . . urgency . . . about this story. We have a chance to do some very important educating. I'm hoping this story will let girls know they have other options."

"What do you mean 'other' options?" Darby pulled her foot up and back until it touched the hem of her shorts. She winced a little.

"Other than abortion, mostly. I'm sure there are girls who get pregnant, panic, and think there's nothing else for them to do. If there are girls out there who want to keep their babies but don't know where to turn, then knowing about Haven House might help them with their decision."

"Keeping a child when you're just a kid yourself is a pretty hard decision," Darby commented as she stretched forward to touch her toes.

"Sure it's hard, but it's also *real*. It's something that has to be faced." Sarah wrinkled her nose. "I don't think it should be shoved under the rug like my aunt Jane does."

"Who's Aunt Jane?"

"My dad's sister. She's a wonderful person, but she absolutely refuses to discuss certain things with her children. She insists that *her* children won't have sex before marriage so there's no reason even to talk about it—or about what might happen if one of them did. I wonder how many girls at Haven House have parents with attitudes like that?"

"Doing the ostrich thing, then? Burying her head in the sand?"

"Exactly. Aunt Jane acts as though if you don't talk about something, it won't happen. My dad is totally different. He believes in talking about everything, including the consequences of the decisions we make. Ignoring issues or problems won't make them go away. That's what my dad says." Sarah turned her wheelchair toward the door. "Ready?"

They moved down the hall to the weight room, a high-tech mirrored space full of forbidding-looking machines. There were two men present, one doing bench presses, the other rowing energetically on a rowing machine. Both were exhaling great huffs of air and gulping furiously as they inhaled.

"Are they all right?" Darby whispered.

"Sure. That's how you do it. Inhale as you relax and exhale as you press. You need oxygen."

Darby looked at the bright red faces. "Looks like they could use even more."

Sarah laughed and wheeled her way to a contraption of weights, benches, and pulleys. "I usually start with a few lat pull-downs," she explained as she maneuvered her wheelchair into place and grasped the long bar with molded rubber handles on either end. "Like this."

Sarah demonstrated the pull and then wrinkled her nose. "Too light." She moved a peg to increase the weight and started again. When she was done, Darby moved to try the station.

"You'll have to get on your knees," Sarah explained. "Pull it down behind your head for ten repetitions. That should be enough to start."

Darby pulled. Nothing moved. Darby gave an unladylike grunt. "Why did it move for you and not for me?"

"Pull harder."

Darby tried again with the same results.

"Looks like we'll have to start you with less weight," Sarah observed. "Pull the peg and move it up a few notches."

When Darby had finally managed to have some success—at a considerably lighter weight than the one Sarah was accustomed to using—she gave a gasp of disbelief. "I never realized how *strong* you are!"

"People never consider the idea that the disabled should be in shape." Sarah was now bench-pressing a considerable amount of weight, and her words came in breathy spurts. "When, actually, we need it *more* than the rest of the population. Otherwise we could sit in our wheelchairs and positively bloat up! Besides, it's fun."

"For you, maybe. It's just about killing me." Darby moved to the slant bench and lay with her feet elevated above her head. Then, in a complete change of topics, she said, "Tell me more about your aunt Jane."

Sarah sighed. "We love her dearly, but we can't convince her to live in the real world sometimes. For example, she'd think that Haven House was all wrong because teenagers shouldn't be having babies. She believes that parents should educate their children to stay chaste until they are married."

"I agree with that," Darby commented, doing a halfhearted sit-up.

"I do too. The difference is that she won't accept the fact that it still happens and there are families who do have to face the issue. She thinks if we ignore sex, it will go away."

"Nothing goes away if you ignore it. Not even a messy room or the dinner dishes—they just attract a bigger mess."

"Exactly. And that's why I'm so excited to be doing this story on Haven House. Rather than ignoring the problem, it's taking responsibility to help the girls who would otherwise 'slip through the cracks.' I'm glad there's somebody willing to help and to train girls who choose to have their babies."

"What does Haven House do about the babies' fathers? And grandparents? Where do they fit in to the picture?"

"I'm anxious to find out. Molly and Josh said they could—"

"Are you *still* talking about that assignment?" a familiar voice asked.

"Shane! Hi. What are you doing here?"

"Oh, he comes here all the time, don't you, Shane?" Sarah said. "He hates following me, though. My weights are always too light for him."

"Hah! You'll have to quit adding pounds soon or I'll hurt myself." He dropped into a molded seat and began to do leg presses. Obviously he and Sarah had shared this machine often.

"I thought you lifted weights at school," Darby said. "I've seen you there."

"I do, but Mom gave me a membership at this club for my birthday. I really like working out here. The equipment is newer and it's usually less crowded."

"Aren't you going to warm up?" Sarah asked.

"I did a few laps around the track. Need some help?"

Sarah was lifting herself from the weight bench into her wheelchair. She was perched rather precariously between the two when Shane spoke.

With a quick shove of her arms, Sarah launched herself back into her wheelchair. "Got it."

She turned to grin at him. "What's the use of lifting weights if I don't lift my *own* weight once in a while?"

"You are totally amazing," Darby mused, then turned to Shane. "Don't you agree?"

"There's no way I would want to get into a fight with Sarah. She'd clobber me."

"Quit it, both of you," Sarah said, blushing. "I like to do the pull-ups, chin-ups, and other upper-body stuff. It makes me feel . . . normal."

"And it's great for keeping Izzy in line," Shane murmured.

Sarah turned as red as her hair. "Quit teasing, Donahue, or I'll have to put *you* in line."

Darby moved to another station and tinkered with the weights. "You've inspired me, Sarah. This is neat. I'll bet if I did this a few times a week, I'd feel better about myself."

"Exactly. My physical therapist got me started. She said that lifting would be good for my self-esteem as well as my health—and she was right." Sarah flexed the muscles in her arm. "I feel safer too."

Shane glanced up sharply. "Why? Has someone been bothering you?"

Sarah smiled sweetly. "No, but thanks for looking like you're willing to be my knight in shining armor. I want to be as free and independent as possible. My customized van helps, and it also means that I can travel alone. It's good to be strong. I can practically fly in this wheelchair if I have to."

"I believe that," Darby said. "I've tried to catch you when you were cruising down the halls at school. If you were on foot, the teachers would accuse you of running!"

"Guess I'd better slow down," Sarah admitted.

"Sometimes, when the hall is almost empty, I do put on the speed." She blushed. "I imagine myself in a race and let go just to feel the wind through my hair—like running, only on wheels."

"Would you really like to race?" Shane asked. "Could you do it around here?"

"Maybe. My dad is looking into a program for wheelchair athletes. If there isn't one, maybe we could start something. It would be great, wouldn't it?"

"Okay, okay, I'll start exercising!" Darby yelped suddenly.

Sarah and Shane turned to stare at her. "What are you talking about?"

"Here I am with two perfectly good legs and arms and I can barely lift a thing! And there's Sarah, in a wheelchair, strong as can be. You've guilted me into this. I'm going to get healthy." She pushed on a weight and gave a groan. "If I don't hurt myself first!"

"I think I'm in love!" Kate drifted into the media room in a haze of happiness.

"And I'm President of the United States," Andrew retorted.

"That's nice," Kate murmured as she sank into the nearest chair with a blissful sigh.

"Who is the unlucky fellow?" Izzy asked. "Anybody we know?"

"No. You don't know him."

"Does he go to Brentwood High?" Molly asked. "And is he cute?"

"No, he doesn't go to Brentwood." Kate's eyes were shining. Always attractive, today she was positively glowing. "And I don't know if he's cute or not."

"Hard to tell, huh?" Izzy frowned. "Not a good sign. It must be love. Usually you only go for the hunks."

"No, no, it's not that I can't tell, it's that I don't *know*. I've never seen him." Kate looked at Izzy as though he were a real moron for not following her statement.

"Then how can you be in love?" Shane asked in his usual matter-of-fact manner. "Have you been watching too much television?"

"Our minds have met," Kate said cryptically. "And it was love at first sight."

"Gray matter meets gray matter," Izzy deduced. "Very romantic. I'll bet those little convoluted brain wrinkles were dancing with joy."

"Make sense, will you?" Molly demanded. "What are you talking about?"

"Steve. His name is Steve." Kate wrote the name in big letters on the front of her notebook. "We met on the Internet last night and we talked for hours. He's from Maryland. He and I think so much alike that it's unbelievable. He's going to fax me his picture today."

"Love in the '90s," Ms. Wright chuckled.

"I don't get it," Julie said. "You're all obsessed

with this computer stuff. Now you're meeting guys on it?"

"You're going to have to break down and learn about computers someday, Julie," Darby said with a smile.

"Not if I can help it. What's wrong with paper, pencils, and telephones, anyway?" Julie had a phobia about machines if they didn't have something to do with drying or curling her hair. "Besides, Kate doesn't know anything about this guy. He could have been lying to her about everything!"

"People do that in person too," Kate answered logically. "At least on the Internet you get to know how someone thinks before you meet physically."

"It's not likely you're going to meet anytime soon," Andrew pointed out. "You aren't exactly in Maryland."

Kate turned her nose in the air and gave a sniff of disdain. "See if I tell you about my on-line romance again. You'll see I'm right when Steve comes to visit me and he is totally cool."

"I can hardly wait," Andrew muttered. "That will be worth a news story!"

"I'm really nervous," Molly said tremulously as she, Sarah, and Josh pulled up in front of the plain brick building that looked like it was built in the 1920s. Only a tiny sign over the front that said *Haven House* identified the structure. It blended unobtrusively into the long block of old apartment buildings.

"Me too," Sarah murmured. "This is weird."

Josh snorted loudly. "*You* feel weird? What about me? I'm a guy! How do you think *I* feel about walking into a home for school-aged mothers?"

"It's kind of depressing looking, isn't it?" Molly said of the dark red brick. "Like a prison."

"Ms. Wright says it's not that way at all. Maybe appearances are deceiving," Josh said hopefully.

They were pleasantly surprised. As the threesome stepped into the foyer of Haven House, they were met by a pinwheel of color and cheerful noise. There was music coming from a nearby room, and two toddlers played together over a pile of colored blocks in the hallway. A young girl who couldn't have been more than fifteen walked toward them carrying a basket of laundry that contained pastel sleepers and tiny white T-shirts. The girl looked at them shyly before turning into one of the rooms.

Almost immediately another girl appeared from the other side of the hall. She, too, looked to be no older than sixteen. Still, with a baby on her hip and a tense, drawn expression on her face, she seemed to be a contradiction—young and old, carefree and full of care, happy yet sad.

"There you are!" The brusk but cheerful voice startled them all. A large and imposing-looking woman was bearing down upon them. Her blue eyes twinkled as she reached them. Her expression was merry. "You must be the students from Brentwood High. Welcome. I'm Mrs. Barry."

The name was familiar to them. According to Ms. Wright, Mrs. Barry was credited with being administrator of Haven House since its beginning.

"Come into the living room," the woman invited. "Let's visit for a moment before we take a tour." She led them into a cozy room decorated in warm, homey colors. There were two couches and several easy chairs arranged into two conversation areas. A small color television played in one corner. Lush green plants decorated every table.

"This is where everyone at Haven House entertains their guests," Mrs. Barry said. "Sometimes it gets pretty crowded, but we don't mind." She studied Sarah, Josh, and Molly. "I assume you have some questions for me before we start our tour."

Josh pulled out a notebook and scanned the first page. "Background information would be very helpful. None of us had even heard of Haven House until recently."

Mrs. Barry nodded. "That's understandable. This is actually a pilot project that a group of churches has undertaken. There are several qualifications which must be met in order to enroll here."

"And they are?" Sarah, too, was taking notes.

"A girl must be in her last stages of pregnancy or already have a child, she must be no older than eighteen, she must not yet have a high school diploma, and in most cases, she should be economically disadvantaged."

"In 'most' cases?" Molly asked.

"Yes. There has been a great demand for what we offer, and occasionally a family that is able to pay tuition wishes to enroll a girl here."

"What, exactly, happens when a girl comes to Haven House?" Sarah asked.

"First she is assigned a volunteer similar to a 'big sister' from the community. This woman is, for all practical purposes, a surrogate mother for the girl. She helps her young mother shop for the baby, teaches her child care, baby-sits, and even helps to work out problems that may arise from school or jobs.

"Our goal at Haven House is to teach young mothers how to care for their babies. An older woman, already a mother, is usually very helpful. Many of the girls and their volunteers become very good friends."

"What else do you teach here?" Molly wondered.

"Nutrition is always stressed. Some girls think they can put diet soft drinks or whatever they are drinking into their child's bottle, and then they wonder why their babies don't thrive. We teach them the importance of cleanliness and why babies do what they do."

"Such as?" Josh asked.

"Cry, fuss, burp, sleep, get sick. When you are a first-time mother at fourteen or fifteen years old, everything is new and frightening. We teach our girls how to be mothers."

"How long can someone stay here?" Sarah asked. She eyed a brightly colored mobile hanging over an empty playpen. Next to it was a storage tower filled with CDs and a stack of magazines for young women.

"As I said, most girls come to us in their last weeks of pregnancy or right after their child is born. These are usually, but not always, girls who have already decided to keep their babies and need a place to stay while they get on their feet. They need to learn mothering skills, finish high school, find a job. There are very few places a girl with an infant or toddler can go for support. We want to provide as much of that as we can."

"So the girls move in and live here until they are ready to move on?" Molly said.

"Yes. We have a full day-care center staffed with professionals. That means the girls can work or go to classes. We help them get their high school equivalency diplomas, line them up with schools, and do some vocational training right here. We have a nurse on staff and a variety of health services available. We want young women to be successful mothers. We do everything we can to get them started on the right foot."

Mrs. Barry smiled at the threesome as they all scribbled notes on the interview. "I know this is a great deal to take in, but once you see the facility and visit with some of the girls, you'll get an idea of how it works."

"Why do you think they do it?" Molly asked abruptly.

"Do what?" Mrs. Barry looked confused.

"Keep their babies instead of giving them up for adoption?"

Mrs. Barry considered for a moment. "Every girl has her own reason, but there are a couple things I've observed. Some girls and their families are morally opposed to adoption and think keeping their baby is what they need to do. I've seen girls who have refused to believe they were pregnant almost until their deliveries. I've also seen girls who come here because, more than anything, they want their child. Any way one looks at it, it's a difficult situation.

"The young women who come here are very brave," Mrs. Barry added.

Molly looked up in surprise. "Brave? I guess I thought coming to Haven House might be more like

. . . running away and hiding."

"These young girls have many things to deal with. Haven House helps them face their issues."

"What kinds of issues?" Josh asked. He was doing rather well considering the topic. Compassionate and gentle, he was genuinely interested in these people in crisis.

"Health, for one. Young, underdeveloped bodies aren't ready for motherhood. Young moms can have high blood pressure or toxemia during pregnancy. Some have had prolonged labor or Cesarean section—surgical delivery of the baby. Occasionally the baby runs into trouble with an abnormal heart rate. Girls come to us exhausted. They don't have time to recover before they are thrust into the world with an infant to care for. Sometimes, for the first week or so, our main goal is to give a girl the opportunity to rest and eat nutritious food."

"Wow," Josh murmured. "I never realized there could be so many problems."

At that moment, gales of laughter erupted somewhere down the hall. Mrs. Barry smiled. "Don't let me give you the wrong idea. Just because there are a lot of problems to overcome and emotional issues to deal with doesn't mean that we don't have happy times, too, here at Haven House." She tipped her head toward the sound of giggling. "Come, meet some of the girls."

There were four girls in the room into which Mrs. Barry led Josh, Molly, and Sarah. One of the girls was obviously very pregnant. In addition, there were three babies in the room—one on the bed, another in a swing seat, and the third lying on a thickly quilted blanket on the floor. If not for the babies, it might have been a teenage slumber party. Everyone turned toward the door as the guests entered.

"These are the students from Brentwood High that I told you about. They work for a student-run cable television program called *Live! From Brentwood High* and are doing a story on Haven House. I know that some of you have volunteered to talk with them."

At that moment, the baby in the swing burst into a wail. One of the girls jumped to her feet and lifted him out of the swing. She held the baby close to her face and sniffed. "Ewww!" she blurted, and the other girls laughed. "Can't stay, Mrs. Barry, a dirty diaper calls." She hurried past them into the hall.

When she'd gone by, Molly waved a hand near her face. "I can smell what she means!" The girls laughed again.

"This is Cheryl," Mrs. Barry said of one of the girls who remained.

"And my son, James." The girl pointed to the baby on the bed, who didn't appear to be more than a few days old.

"I'm Jane," said the other girl. "And this is Rachel." The baby on the floor kicked her legs and waved her arms as if in response to the introduction.

The third girl, the pregnant one, did not look up.

Instead, her eyes remained riveted on the floor.

"Meredith, aren't you going to say hello?" Mrs. Barry asked gently.

"Hello."

"Meredith just joined us at Haven House."

"Her boyfriend lied to her," Cheryl said matter-of-factly. "He told her he loved her, but he was engaged to somebody else the whole time he was seeing her."

Sarah and Molly did all they could to suppress gasps of surprise. Meredith never moved.

"Now she doesn't know what to do. Jane and I are trying to tell her that she'd better start making some plans. She can't hide out forever. Now she's quit school and doesn't have a job, so she's here." Suddenly Cheryl's blunt recital ceased, and she put her arm around Meredith's bowed shoulders. "We'll help you get through it. Lots of us have big problems. We'll make it."

Molly, Josh, and Sarah followed Mrs. Barry out of the room, leaving Meredith and her two friends.

Molly's eyes were huge as she stammered, "Is . . . is that all true? About her boyfriend and having no place to go?"

"I'm afraid so. Sometimes girls think that giving a guy what he wants will draw them closer. As you can see, that often backfires. Fortunately, we have wonderful counselors on staff to help the girls work through their problems."

"And a church does this?" Molly asked.

"Several churches sponsor Haven House. It's one

of the finest expressions of Christ's love I've ever experienced. Much as He hates sin, He always loves the sinner. We were told to go out and feed the hungry and clothe the naked and to love others as we love ourselves. Haven House does all that."

"Do you have a church in here?" Josh looked at the seemingly endless hallways.

"We have a chapel—and services in the dining room on Sundays. The girls enjoy our contemporary service, and they seem to gain strength from the messages. The Bible is a very helpful guide for young women who are feeling lost in chaos and confusion."

Mrs. Barry glanced at her watch. "I don't like to rush you, but I have another appointment. As I told your instructor Ms. Wright, several of the girls are willing, even eager, to talk to you. Since they are occupied with school or work most of the day, it would be best if you talked to them in the late afternoon or early evening. You might want to come back several times, depending on the length of your interviews. Would that be a problem?"

All three shook their heads in unison, glad that the efficient Mrs. Barry had taken some of the decision making out of their hands. This story was already overwhelming, and they hadn't yet begun.

After saying polite goodbyes to Mrs. Barry, Josh, Molly, and Sarah escaped into the late afternoon light.

Molly sank against Sarah's wheelchair as if she might need it too. "My head is spinning!" she blurted. "Did you look at those girls? Really look at them, I mean? They were our age!"

"That's what Haven House is about, silly," Josh chided.

"I know, but I guess it just didn't sink in until I saw it for myself. They're so *young*!" She pushed herself away from Sarah's wheelchair but then dropped down in front of it on the sidewalk, curling her legs under herself. "Babies. Jobs. Broken hearts. Wow! I guess this assignment is going to open our eyes to a thing or two."

"What time is it?" Molly asked. She'd been pacing the floor of the media room for what seemed like ages.

"Two minutes after the last time you asked," Andrew Tremaine said with a yawn. He was handsome at six-feet-two with dark hair and eyes blue as oceans, but his attitude was flippant. "Why don't you just settle down? You're making it hard for me to think."

"Don't blame that on her, Tremaine," Jake Saunders chided, accustomed to keeping Andrew's huge ego in line. "If you can't think, it's your own fault."

Jake scraped his sandy blond hair from his eyes and smiled one of his charming smiles, revealing the one slightly crooked tooth in his otherwise perfect mouth. If Kate wanted "hunks," there were two right here in this room.

"Quiet!" Molly growled. "I've got enough problems without getting flack from you two."

"She's touchy today," Julie commented to Kate as they sat at a long table nearby. "Must not have gotten her beauty sleep."

"Will you all *quit it*? Can't you see I'm a nervous wreck?" Molly threw her hands in the air. Her curly blond hair flew wildly around her face and her cheeks grew pink. Once again she began stalking up and down the floor.

"What's the big deal?" Darby Ellison asked. "You've done interviews before. Besides, Josh and Sarah are going too. It's not as though you have to do this alone. The people at Haven House can't be that scary. You said the administrator was really nice."

"That's not it. I just feel so uncomfortable asking questions about such private matters. 'Why have you decided to keep your baby?' 'Where does the baby's father fit into all of this?' 'How do you like living at Haven House?' I'd be upset if the tables were turned and *I* was being interviewed!"

"But they all agreed to talk to us," Sarah pointed out softly. "They were told why we wanted to talk to them. Mrs. Barry said the girls were glad to help out if they could educate others."

"Still, it feels nasty." Molly drifted to where Josh was helping Gary Richmond pack camera equipment. "Don't you think so, Josh?"

Josh's dark brown eyes turned solefully to Molly. "Don't ask. I can't believe I'm even doing this. I feel like a mouse at a cat convention in that place. I've never seen a guy—except me—in Haven House. I can't think of anything that might make me feel more ill at ease!"

Gary grinned. "Get used to it if you want to be a

photographer or journalist. We're always sticking our noses into places that feel uncomfortable."

"How do you do it, Gary?" Josh asked. "How do you get used to seeing people hurt and not being able to help them?"

They all knew what Josh was referring to. Gary had been on assignment in Bosnia and the Gulf War. He'd done a dramatic portrayal of orphans in Romania. He'd seen a great deal of pain and suffering before he'd come to Brentwood High to teach with his friend Rosie Wright and, as he explained, "To be around people who aren't starving, dying, or being blown up."

Ms. Wright chose that moment to enter. Her hair was anchored to the top of her head with two sticks that looked vaguely like chopsticks, and she wore a loose blue tunic belted with something that resembled twine. "Okay, what's happening here?"

"Gary and Josh are packing equipment, Sarah is waiting patiently, and Molly is having a nervous breakdown," Darby answered.

Ms. Wright turned to Molly. "Nervous?"

"The worst. What if these girls get mad and tell us to go home and mind our own business?"

"Then that's what you'll have to do. Or find others who *will* talk to you. The hallmark of a successful reporter is persistence."

"Then I'll never be very good. I feel as if I'm intruding." Molly sighed. "But I guess I'll have to learn sometime."

"Good attitude." Ms. Wright put down the book she was carrying and turned to Sarah. "What's your game plan for today?"

"We can't interview everyone in one visit," Sarah said, ever the organizer for the group, "so we'll go back as many times as necessary—if we can only fit in one girl a day after her work or schooling is finished, then that's what we'll do. Mrs. Barry suggested that might be the least disruptive."

"Why should it matter?" Kate questioned.

"Some girls will bring their babies to the interviews. If we do only one or two interviews at a time, then not everyone will have to get their baby ready at once."

"What about equipment?" Jake asked, eyeing the pile of stuff accumulating near Josh and Gary.

"There's a sun-room at Haven House that will be ours to use as long as we need it. We can leave the equipment there."

"This is going to be a big flop, I just know it!" Molly moaned, pacing again.

"Now what?" Julie asked sharply, impatient with Molly's theatrics.

"Mrs. Barry suggested talking to the girls with not only their babies, but also their *parents*."

"Sort of a multigenerational gabfest," Andrew said sarcastically. "Sounds like a *lot* of fun."

"No wonder you're nervous. That sounds like it would be very hard," Darby sympathized.

"Hard? More like impossible. I'm not sure I want

to talk about this with my own parents, let alone someone else's!"

"Really?" Sarah spoke. "You wouldn't discuss this subject with your own family?"

"My mom, but I'm not sure I'd be comfortable with my stepdad," Molly said.

"Maybe that's the problem," Sarah murmured. Everyone turned to look at her.

"I mean," she continued, "that perhaps the girls at Haven House *haven't* had anyone to talk to and that's part of the reason they are where they are now. If you're feeling lonely, confused, or pressured to have sex and there's no one to discuss it with . . ."

"Oh, Sarah, you're always trying to get into someone else's brain and figure out what that person is thinking," Julie said. "Besides, the parents aren't going to want to talk to you either. Why should they talk to strangers—crummy little high school kids—about this big deal in their daughter's life?"

"Thanks a bunch. You've made me feel much better," Molly said sarcastically.

"I think Julie's wrong." Shane Donahue spoke for the first time. He'd been so quiet everyone had forgotten he was in the room. "Maybe some parents will want to do what they can to turn a difficult situation into one that teaches other kids something. You know, give a warning or something." Shane flushed, looking as though his outburst had cost him a great deal. "Then again, maybe not."

"Good point!" Sarah said enthusiastically. "We

want an informative show. The more viewpoints we have, the better."

"How do we get into these messes?" Andrew inquired to no one in particular. "Couldn't we do an *easy* story just once? Why do we have to research all these tough issues—school-aged mothers, handicapped teenagers . . ."

"Because that's what people want to see. Nobody cares if we do a show on new hairstyles or how to mow your lawn. Would *you* watch that?" Jake asked.

"Maybe, if it were my hair or my lawn we were talking about," Andrew said flippantly.

"What would it take to get you to watch *this* show?" Julie asked. "*Your* baby?"

Andrew scowled. "That's not funny!"

"No, but it's a great idea!" Izzy exclaimed.

"*Andrew* has a baby?" Josh looked up from what he was doing, puzzled. He hadn't been paying much attention to the conversation until this point. Everyone in the room burst out laughing.

"Go back to work, Josh," Jake ordered. "You're not helping."

Josh shrugged and obeyed.

"What'd you mean by that?" Andrew asked Julie. He was still scowling.

"Just that we should be interviewing the fathers of these babies too."

"Do you think they'd agree?" Kate asked. "It might be pretty embarrassing or uncomfortable for them."

"All we can do is ask," Sarah replied. "It seems to me that they'd better start taking some responsibility for their behavior—especially when there's a child involved."

"Oh, Sarah," Julie said. "Come down off your cloud. Not everyone is as concerned about 'responsibility' as you are."

"No? Maybe not, but everyone *should* be. That's what we should be saying in this program. You can't carelessly bring a new little life into this world and then pretend it doesn't exist." Sarah flushed. It was evident that she felt very strongly about this. "I've thought about it a lot. When people have a child, they bring a whole new soul into this world—a soul that will exist throughout eternity. Somebody has to take responsibility!"

"Only *you* would look at it like that," Kate muttered. "The weird thing is, you're beginning to make sense. Now, that's really scary!"

Sarah smiled, recognizing the victory behind Kate's backhanded compliment. Being the only Christian in the group wasn't easy, but sometimes when she least expected it something she said or believed or lived sank in and left a lasting impression.

"How are you going to do it?" Shane asked, eyeing the list of equipment Josh was working with.

"We're going to have each girl tell her story to Sarah. She's a great interviewer and a good listener. People seem to *want* to talk to Sarah," Molly explained. "After all, wouldn't *you* be willing to tell Sarah your problems?"

"Good thing Andrew's not on this assignment," Julie said snidely. "Nobody wants to talk to him."

Andrew didn't even bother to react. The teasing that went on around the media room was usually best ignored.

"Josh," Kate called, "how did you get so lucky as to stay behind the camera?"

Josh grinned but his smile faded when Gary said, "I think Josh's luck may have run out."

"What do you mean?" Josh turned to Gary.

"If they're going to interview fathers, they'd probably be more comfortable with you."

"I never thought about that," Josh muttered. "Guess that means I'd better get a haircut."

Darby and Sarah both burst out laughing. "Do you think anyone will be able to tell?" They often teased Josh about his tight black curls and the fact that his hair usually looked the same whether he cut it or not.

"I suppose that means you get every other job," Julie said to Molly.

"Right. I'll be the stage manager."

"Well, then, Miss Stage Manager," Gary said, "you'd better get this show on the road, or we'll be late for our first interview."

Molly let out a small screech and clutched her stomach. "I'm so nervous I'm going to throw up!"

Andrew stood up and walked toward the exit. "All I can say is that I'm glad I'm not working on this story. I'd probably be in charge of cleaning up after Molly!"

Gary shook his head and hoisted a bag to his shoulder. "You'll have to be sick in the car, Molly. The show must go on."

Mrs. Barry was waiting for them at the door to Haven House. "Good. You're on time."

She eyed the impressive-looking equipment that Gary, Josh, and Molly were unloading before turning to Sarah. "You've created quite a stir around here, you know."

"Us?"

"Yes. Your upcoming television show has been the primary topic of conversation around here."

"Why?"

"Because I asked the girls to decide who should be interviewed. Some of them, of course, want to protect their privacy and declined immediately. Others rather like the idea of telling their story." Mrs. Barry smiled. "Some want to do some good by educating other young women to the benefits and pitfalls of being a teenager raising a baby. Others just want to see themselves on TV."

"I hope we haven't caused any problems for you," Sarah said, concern creasing her forehead.

"No, not really. We use every opportunity we have to discuss the futures of these girls. This has actually been a good tool for conversation."

Mrs. Barry led them down the hall to the bright, pleasant room filled with sunlight and plants. Furniture had already been moved to accommodate the filming.

"Mrs. Barry, this is Gary Richmond," Sarah said by way of introduction. Gary nodded politely and continued to give Josh setup directions. As always, Gary liked to fade into the background when the students were working. It was easy to forget Gary was present unless he chose to remind them.

Just as Josh finished clipping a mike to the lapel of Sarah's jacket, a pale, waifish girl with light blond hair hanging softly around her face entered the room. She was very slender, a quality accentuated by her high cheekbones. She couldn't have been more than fifteen or sixteen, but it was obvious that she would be a real beauty someday. Her eyes, a bright clear blue, took in the room, the guy tinkering with the camera, the redheaded girl in the wheelchair, the blonde with the amazingly frizzy hair, and the man dressed in faded denim and wearing a ponytail.

"Hello?" It was a question, not a greeting. There was a fragile quality about the girl that made her appear as though she might break in a strong wind, but her step was sure and steady as she approached. She carried a bundle of blankets in her arms.

Sarah immediately rolled her wheelchair toward the girl. "Tammy?"

The girl nodded.

"Hello. I'm Sarah and this is Molly. Josh and Gary are the pair working with the cameras. We're from *Live! From Brentwood High.*"

"I know. Mrs. Barry told me about you." She clutched the blankets as they began to squirm. Almost as an afterthought, she added, "This is Aimee."

Tammy peeled away the blankets to reveal a tiny, frail-looking infant whose face was screwing into a dreadful pucker. The baby squawked a complaint.

"She sounds like a bird!" Molly blurted, then blushed to the roots of her hair. "A *nice* bird. I mean, sounding like a bird isn't that bad . . . I mean . . ."

Sarah and Tammy stared at Molly for a moment, and then both burst out laughing.

"It's okay," Tammy said. "She *does* sound like a bird. I've thought so myself."

"May I hold her?" Sarah asked. "If you wouldn't mind, that is."

"Sure." Tammy willingly laid the bundle in Sarah's arms.

"Oh!" Sarah gasped as the baby kicked its feet. "She's wiggly—and strong!"

"Why don't we get you ready for the interview while Sarah is holding Aimee?" Molly asked. She directed Tammy toward a chair with a mike draped over the arm. When Tammy was seated, Molly clipped it to the placket of her blouse.

"You understand, then, what we're going to do here today?" Molly asked.

Tammy nodded. "You want to interview high-school-aged mothers who plan to keep their babies. You want to know why we did it and how we plan to manage. Mrs. Barry told us." She glanced around the room. "It's neat in here, looks like a television studio."

"That's the idea," Josh said, speaking for the first time. He held a release paper in his hands. "We'd like you to sign this. It says you agreed to talk to us and that we can use the interview for our cable TV show."

Sarah glanced at the paper and signed it with the pen Josh handed her. She studied her name and then impulsively added on the line beneath "and Aimee."

"Do you like how it's spelled?" she asked. "A-I-M-E-E. Everybody thought I should spell her name A-M-Y, but I wanted it to be more special."

"It's very nice," Sarah assured her. She looked down at the baby. "And she's beautiful."

Tammy held out her hands as Sarah transferred the infant into her arms. "I know. I think so too. Sometimes I can't quit looking at her. She's so perfect that it's hard to believe she's mine." Tammy held the baby tightly, close to her chest. "She's the first thing I've ever been able to call my own."

"Thing?" Josh muttered under his breath. "A baby's not a 'thing.' "

Gary silenced him with a poke in the ribs and a dirty look. Josh rolled his eyes and made a show of tinkering with a camera that was already set.

Molly, who was in charge of making sure things ran smoothly, cleared her throat and said, "Let's just get started. Sarah will be conducting the interview, Tammy. She's the one who's prepared the questions. We really appreciate your agreeing to talk to us and willingness to be honest. I know this can't be easy, but we'll try to make it as smooth as possible."

"Oh, I don't mind," Tammy said. "I wanted to come. I've never been on television before. Besides, Mrs. Barry told us we could have a copy of the video. That way I'll have something to show Aimee when she grows up."

Sarah and Molly exchanged a look. Tammy was a very strange combination of innocence and maturity, and she slipped from one to the other with startling ease.

"Let's get going," Gary said. "We'd better get some footage before everyone is tired."

Spurred into action, Sarah rolled into place, clipped on her mike, and began the brief introductory words she'd planned. Then, with a warm smile, she turned to Tammy.

"How old is Aimee?" she asked.

"Two weeks today." Tammy, acting as though she'd been on camera dozens of times before, peeled away Aimee's blanket and held her toward the camera. The baby made sucking motions with her lips and managed with some difficulty to plug her thumb into her mouth.

"You're fifteen, Tammy. How does it feel to be a mom?"

Tammy pondered the question thoughtfully. "How does it *feel*? I guess I haven't had much time to feel anything. I go to classes, take care of Aimee, and sleep whenever I can. Sometimes I think I'm more robot than human."

She chewed on her lower lip as if Sarah's question had disturbed her. "It's weird to hear yourself being called a 'mom.' Moms are adults—the ones who make the rules and drive you crazy. They are the ones who are always telling you what to do and how to do it. And now I am one. . . ." There was amazement in her voice.

"Did you have any idea what to expect?" Sarah asked.

"I thought I did. I've done lots of baby-sitting—at least I did before I got a boyfriend. That was easy enough. It didn't seem like a real big deal to raise kids. Feed them. Play with them. Put them to bed. It shouldn't be so hard, should it?"

Suddenly and unexpectedly, Tammy's eyes filled with tears. "I guess people tried to tell me it was harder than that, but I wouldn't listen."

She wiped the tears away with the back of her hand and looked embarrassed. She glanced at Josh. "Do we have to leave that in?"

"We'll be editing later."

"Oh, okay." Tammy frowned. "Actually, Mrs. Barry says the reason it's so hard is that I've never been a parent before. She says that I'll make mistakes, but I'll also do some things right and that I have to remember that it's perfectly natural." She looked lovingly at the baby who had fallen asleep on her lap. "It's just that I want to do everything just right for her."

"Are you frightened sometimes?" Sarah asked softly. Josh and Molly both looked up. That question hadn't been planned.

"Terrified." Tammy stroked the baby's forehead. "I didn't realize until I held her in my arms that she wasn't some kind of fantastic toy that I could put down when I got tired of playing with her. She's still going to be mine when we're both old ladies—mother and daughter." Her eyes grew round. "I'd just never thought about it before."

Tammy was talking to herself, and Sarah had grown very still. Josh and Gary seemed frozen behind the camera.

"I just want to do what's right, what's best for her, you know?" A tear slipped down her cheek. "Sometimes I get so scared. . . ."

Sarah laid a gentle hand on Tammy's arm. "Tell me, what's the *best* thing about taking care of her?"

Molly made a small sound at the back of the room, but Gary shushed her. Sarah's script had totally gone out the window, but they were getting some very powerful footage. Sarah seemed to know instinctively what to ask next.

"The best?" Tammy brightened. "Feeding her.

Definitely that. Her little mouth works, and I can hold her close and rock her. She's happy and then I'm happy. I love it when she burps. It's this great big sound coming out of this little tiny girl. She relaxes then, and usually goes to sleep. I change her diaper and rock her some more. Sometimes I wish there wasn't anything in this world but Aimee and me and a rocking chair."

Tammy appeared pensive. "Funny, though, because the *best* things can also be the *worst*."

"What do you mean?" Sarah asked.

"Even though I love to feed and rock her, I have to be doing it over and over again. She doesn't sleep very long—just naps. Sometimes I get so exhausted I just wish she'd sleep eight hours in a row so I could too! Now I have to fit everything into those hours—homework, laundry, cleaning my room, sleep and, pretty soon, my part-time job. How am I going to do it all?"

Again, tears came into Tammy's eyes. This time she didn't try to brush them away. Instead, she gave a wobbly smile. "Sorry. I think my hormones are out of whack. Mrs. Barry says it's called 'postpartum blues.' It's lousy."

"What can you do about it?" Sarah asked, feeling very much over her head in this conversation—child-care, exhaustion, depression—these weren't the fairy tale parts of having a child!

"Time will take care of it. I talked to the doctor, and he said it would improve. Sometimes it helps just to look at Aimee." Tammy shifted the bundle. "No one has ever loved me the way she does. She wants *me.* Sometimes she'll grab my finger and hold on so tight I can hardly believe it. Every day she does something new. I can't believe she's mine."

"Tammy," Sarah said softly, "what do your parents think of Aimee?"

Tammy's look hardened, and her eyes darted away from Sarah's gentle gaze. "She's my baby. What does it matter?"

"They're her grandparents. I just wondered what they thought about their daughter raising a child at such a young age."

"They don't like it. They think I should have given her up for adoption. That's why I'm here—because I want to take care of Aimee without their help."

"They won't give it?"

"Oh, they would, but I'd hear about it forever—about my 'big mistake.' At least here I don't get lectures. Haven House is a real 'haven.' At least we aren't on the street and I can go to school."

"How long can you stay here?"

"Until I get settled. There are girls here with toddlers. Some have gone out and come back again. A couple have even started to work here permanently."

"How much does it cost?" Sarah asked.

"That's the best part. As long as we work here and stay in school, we can stay for free. Once you get a job, you have to pay for day-care, but it's cheap."

"Then who pays for all of this?" Sarah marveled.

"Churches. We're one of their 'missions.' There are fund raisers, and girls whose parents can afford it pay a tuition. Sometimes people give donations because they think it's a good idea to teach girls how to be good parents. When I grow up and get a job, I'm going to give back everything I can."

When she grew up. . . .

The comment was not lost on any of the *Live!* crew. Aimee and her mother would be growing up together. Two children alone together.

Molly turned away and dug into the pocket of her jeans for a tissue. When she was done dabbing at her eyes, she noticed that Josh, too, had tears welling at the corners of his deep brown eyes. Even Gary, who had seen so much of the world, looked touched.

Only Sarah seemed completely in control. She finished the interview with the promise that she and Tammy would talk again.

As Tammy gathered together the baby and blankets she said, "Now you *promise* that I'll get a copy of this tape? I don't have money for a baby book, you know, but I thought that this would be a really neat thing for Aimee to have when she grows up."

With thanks and promises, they sent her out of the room. Quietly Sarah removed the mike from her lapel and laid it on a nearby stool. Josh covered the camera and turned off the lights. They locked up and left Haven House without speaking.

It wasn't until they were all in the parking lot that

Josh blurted, "I didn't think this was going to be so *hard*!"

"Sometimes life is hard," Gary said, giving him a pat on the back. "And kids trying to raise babies definitely fits into that category."

Unable to get Tammy and the haunting, wistful quality of her interview out of their minds, they went home.

"You should have seen her, Darby," Molly was saying. "She was so thin and frail and looked even younger than she was."

"And the way she looked at that baby!" Sarah added. "Love just radiated from her eyes, but . . ."

"But what?"

"I don't know how she's going to make it," Sarah said bluntly. "I couldn't."

"There was something so . . . sad . . . about her," Molly said. "And the baby was so tiny. I haven't been able to get either one of them out of my mind."

Darby looked from Molly to Sarah and back again. "I don't remember either of you ever being so upset about a story before—unless it was the one we did on sexual harassment." Darby referred to a time when Molly's employer was being very unethical.

"I just keep trying to imagine what it would be like to be Tammy. She's younger than we are and already a mom. Everything she does from now on has to be planned around Aimee. How will she ever have a *life*? I keep wondering if she'll be strong enough to do it."

"What choice does she have?" Sarah asked bluntly. "She's already made her decision."

"Let's not talk about this anymore," Molly pleaded. "Somebody, quick, change the subject."

"I agree with Molly," Sarah said. "I have some questions about my homework that I really need to ask. Besides, I can do what I need to do for Tammy and her baby when I get home."

Molly looked at her curiously. "What's that?"

"Pray, of course."

One by one the staff of *Live! From Brentwood High* drifted into the media room after school. It had become the unofficial hangout of all the members of the group, and even when there was no work to be done, Chaos Central was where everyone could be found.

Jake and Darby were the only two busy with a specific assignment.

"What are you working on?" Julie asked curiously. She flipped her straight dark hair away from her face and peered over Jake's shoulder.

"Why, do you want to help?" Jake asked, annoyed at being interrupted.

"Of course not. Just curious."

"We're working on that survey we did of junior high kids. The 'Teens for the Twenty-First Century' story."

"I'm not sure I like that story," Julie said with a yawn. "What's so different about them? The twenty-first century isn't very far away."

"Wouldn't it be weird to graduate in the year 2000?" Andrew said. "What number would you wear on your letter jacket, zero-zero?"

"Actually, it's quite interesting," Darby said. "I'd forgotten what it's like to be fourteen."

"That's because it was such a long time ago," Andrew joked. "You're an old lady now."

"Who cares how it is to be thirteen?" Julie huffed. "Certainly not me!"

"I do," Sarah said gently. "What have they said so far?"

Darby picked up a sheaf of papers and skimmed the words. "Pizza is still everyone's most favorite food. Sports and music are the big interests."

"What a yawn." Julie still wasn't intrigued.

"The big change is computers," Jake said. "Almost everyone we talked to not only took computer classes at school, but many also had one at home. They're using e-mail and surfing the Internet. Everybody liked computer games."

"I've never been on the Internet," Julie said. "Isn't it hard to use?"

"Not for the teenagers of the twenty-first century," Darby said. "I guess you're just getting old and out of touch."

Julie sniffed but looked worried. "I guess I'll take desktop publishing next semester. I suppose I have to start somewhere. Can you believe it? Behind the times? Me?"

"Weird," Josh said out of the blue.

"Who? Julie?" Andrew asked sweetly.

"Listen to yourselves—worrying about 'keeping up' with younger kids, not missing out on some big trend. Now compare that to the story Molly, Sarah, and I are working on about Haven House."

"That's different," Julie said. "Those girls are mothers."

"Exactly," Josh retorted. "But those girls *aren't* different from us—except that because they are mothers they have more to worry about than what underclassmen are doing or how to get on the Internet. They've got families to take care of."

"Ewwww!" Kate squeaked. "When you say it like that, it sounds so . . . permanent!"

"It is permanent. Your parents still have to take care of you, don't they? And your grandparents probably worry about *both* you and your parents."

"I never thought about it that way," Kate admitted.

"Me either," Julie said. "I guess we're lucky we don't have all the responsibilities that the girls at Haven House do. Of course, we don't have those cute little babies either. . . ."

"Babies grow. Look at you. I'll bet you were cute once too."

Julie gave Andrew a dirty look, but a little moan from Molly interrupted what she might have said.

"What's wrong with you?" Julie turned to Molly.

"Major mega-nerves. I dread going to Haven

House tomorrow. Who knows what kind of interview we'll have?"

Chrissie Banks' hair alone would make a Technicolor television special. It was burgundy—or at least fifty percent of it was. Coal black at the roots, her hair color then faded into the purplish burgundy hue before ending at the tips in a peroxided yellow blond. One hunk of hair was tied up in a shabby-looking ponytail that sprouted from the top of her head like a whale's spout. Gaudy silver-and-black earrings dangled from her multi-pierced ears to her shoulders. She wore black leggings, an oversized black T-shirt, and sandals.

Chrissie blew a bubble with the wad of gum in her mouth before saying, "Hi. Mrs. Barry said you were waiting for me. What do you want to know?"

Sarah was the first one to gather her composure. "Did she tell you we were taping interviews for a student-run television show?"

"Yeah. Cool." Chrissie's rainbow hair bounced. She ran blueberry-colored nails through her bangs. "Does that mean I'll be on television for sure?"

"Definitely," Josh choked. "You'll be great. Colorful."

Chrissie evaluated his comment for a moment before deciding not to take issue with it. She gave a huge chomp on her gum and said, "So what are we waiting for? Christmas?"

Josh dived behind the camera before he could put his foot in his mouth again, and Molly patted the chair Chrissie was to sit in.

Chrissie arranged her T-shirt around her hips, adjusted her posture, and struck a prim pose. It reminded Sarah of a leather-clad biker type going to her first tea party.

"She doesn't look very 'motherly,' does she?" Molly whispered to Josh. "I wonder why she wanted to keep her baby."

"We can't judge," Josh whispered back. "Maybe Sarah will ask her."

At that moment, Chrissie was studying Sarah's wheelchair with undisguised interest. "What happened to you?"

"I got hit by a car," Sarah answered, unbothered by Chrissie's blunt question.

"Rotten luck. Will you ever get out?"

"Probably not."

"How do you feel about it?" Chrissie asked. "I'd be bummed out."

"I've accepted it," Sarah said, "but I get 'bummed out' sometimes too."

"What do guys think of it?" Chrissie ventured. "Like, can you get a date?"

Sarah's laughter sang through the room. "I date a very nice guy, thank you. But who's supposed to be doing the interview? You or me?"

Chrissie grinned. "I think I'd be good on television. I watch the news all the time." She touched her head. "I'd have to finish growing out my hair, though. Those newscasters look pretty conservative to me."

She tugged at the tips of her hair. "This platinum thing was a *big* mistake. I did it myself with a bottle of peroxide. I just wanted to see what the tips would look like blond. Not good, huh?"

By now, even Gary was grinning. Chrissie had captured them all with her off-the-wall approach and frank conversation.

Sarah, who had sharp interviewing instincts, seemed to know that Chrissie was not the kind of interviewee that needed to be handled with kid gloves. Just the opposite, in fact. Sarah asked the question which opened the fountain of Chrissie's life.

"Why don't you tell me a little about your background," Sarah said. "How you got to Haven House and about your baby."

"My background? Me? You think anybody cares about that?"

When Sarah nodded, Chrissie took a deep breath and plunged in.

"I moved out of my mom's house and in with my boyfriend 'cause my mom didn't want me there anymore. I was an 'inconvenience,' she said. What she meant was that her new boyfriend didn't like me. They're getting married and wanted me out. It probably wasn't such a good idea, though." Chrissie made a rueful face. "'Cause I got pregnant and now there are *two* of us 'inconveniences.' "

Sarah swallowed thickly. This was a cruel and

shocking story for her. She'd been loved and sheltered all her life. Were there really moms like Chrissie's out there? Obviously.

Chrissie, oblivious to Sarah's distress, plowed ahead. "My boyfriend's no prize either. He's pretty lazy. He mooches off his mother a lot, but he's got an apartment with his brother, so I have a place to go." A fleeting look of pain crossed Chrissie's features.

"Is there more?" Sarah asked softly.

Chrissie looked at her sharply. She had completely forgotten the running camera and the spellbound crew behind it. "He hits me sometimes, that's all."

"And you put up with it?" Sarah was shocked.

Chrissie shrugged her shoulders as if it weren't much of a problem. "Oh, I can handle him. I don't worry about it."

"But what about the baby?"

"Oh, he won't touch her. He's only seen her a couple times since I came to Haven House. If he did try anything . . . let's just say he knows better. Besides, I'll never leave her alone. I'll take good care of her."

"So you haven't considered giving your baby up for adoption at all?"

Chrissie's eyes narrowed. "No way! She's mine. I had her. How do I know she'd get a good home?"

Sarah bit her lip. It would do no good to point out that it was doubtful that this poor infant would get a good home under the current circumstances either. Chrissie was as defensive as a mother lion.

"How will you support her?"

Chrissie frowned. "At first I thought I'd just do like my mom did and go on welfare, but lately, since I came here, I've been thinking about finishing high school and getting a job." She crossed her arms over her chest. "I'm pretty smart when I try. Maybe I could go to college." Her face creased in a smile. "Wouldn't that be a kick? *Me*, a teacher or something?"

While Chrissie pondered that idea, Sarah had a few thoughts of her own. She had no doubt that Chrissie was smart. And brave. And strangely personable. But when everything else was against her, was that enough?

Mrs. Barry had briefed the crew on each of the girls. About Chrissie she had said, "The girl is bright, big-hearted, and full of spirit. And her life is a total mess right now. But if anyone can make it, Chrissie will, even though it will be an uphill climb."

Uphill climb? Sarah thought to herself. Chrissie was climbing Mt. Everest!

"Whew!" Josh muttered after Chrissie had breezed out of the room. "Was she really our age?"

"A life like that would do it to you," Molly said. "My life is beginning to look pretty good. At least my stepdad wants me to live with them!"

She looked at her clipboard. "We've got one more interview lined up for today."

"Can it be any more interesting than the last one?" Josh commented. He folded a stick of gum into his mouth and chewed thoughtfully.

"I hope not," Sarah sighed. "Well, let's do it!"

It was odd, Sarah decided, not knowing what would come up in the next interview. A thumbnail sketch of each girl hardly prepared her for the real thing. These were interesting, complex, burdened people. It was becoming clear that while some were lost and unwanted, others were much loved and supported.

Karla Kerns was one of the first category.

Her dishwater-blond hair was cut short and boyishly. Her green eyes were large and wary and held an expression of fear and confusion. She was sixteen and a half but looked younger. In the right clothing, she could easily have passed for twelve or thirteen. Her baby was four weeks old, and Karla's primary goal at the moment was to finish high school.

In spite of Sarah's and Molly's fussing over her and Josh's feeble attempt at jokes, Karla continued to look terrified.

Sarah wondered why on earth Karla had even agreed to speak to them.

Hoping to ease her into the interview, Sarah began with what she hoped was an easy question. "What brought you to Haven House?"

Sarah was not prepared for the tears that came to Karla's eyes or the strong expression of emotion to her face. "I had nowhere else to go."

She took a swipe at her eyes with the back of her hand. "Sorry. I get emotional sometimes. I don't know what I would have done without this place or my friends here." Karla gave a wavery smile. "You interviewed Chrissie, didn't you?"

Sarah nodded.

"She was great to me when I arrived. She's a little . . . rough . . . around the edges, but her heart is good."

"You said you had no place to go, Karla, other than Haven House," Sarah said gently. "Would you like to explain?"

Karla's gaze flickered, and it seemed as though, in that moment, she was thinking of something very sad and distant. "Would you like to see his picture?"

"Your baby's?"

"No. My boyfriend." Karla handed Sarah a picture. "He died three months ago."

"Died?" Sarah echoed.

"At work. He was in construction. There was a cave-in. . . ." Karla shuddered. "I didn't believe it at first. When it finally sank in that he was never coming back, I didn't want to live either."

Sarah reached out and put her hand on Karla's arm. The girl seemed to take strength from the touch and continued. "I tried to commit suicide. I gathered all the pills I could find and took them. I wanted to forget everything, to not exist any longer, but the doctors wouldn't let me. They saved my life.

"When I was well enough, I was moved into the psychiatric ward at the hospital. It was there that I decided that I needed to live. I was carrying Randy's baby. Even if he didn't live, the baby could. That's why I'm here. I need to get an education and find a job. Haven House can help me do that."

"What about your family?" Sarah asked, appalled that this young woman was so alone.

"They said I had to chose between them and Randy. I chose Randy. They were very hurt and angry. I can't go back now. I talk to my sister sometimes when she's at home alone. My dad moved all my stuff out of my room and turned it into a TV room. They even changed the carpet. I guess they didn't want anything that would remind them of me."

"You don't have to talk about your parents, Karla," Sarah said.

"It's okay," Karla said as she composed herself. "This show is going to be seen by lots of kids, right? Maybe somebody else is going through the same thing. If I talk about my problems, maybe they won't feel so alone."

"You are very brave," Sarah said with genuine admiration in her voice.

"I don't want to be. It's just that I don't have any choice. My parents are making a big mistake. My baby and I will be all right if only . . ." Momentary terror flashed in Karla's eyes, and her show of strength crumbled. She began to weep.

Forgetting everything but the sobbing girl, Josh and Molly both stepped forward. Josh knelt at Karla's feet and Molly put a hand on her shoulders and murmured sounds of comfort.

Finally, when the storm of tears had subsided,

Karla looked up at them and whispered, "I'm so scared."

"Have you talked to your parents?" Josh slipped in. "Told them how much you hurt. Maybe they could—"

"It's not that. It's the baby." Karla dug in the pocket of her jeans for a tissue. Molly picked an entire box off the table and handed it to her. "See, I'm afraid that when I took all those pills, I might have hurt the baby. I lived in terror every day until she was born. I thought maybe she'd be deformed—no toes or fingers or head or something. I wondered how I'd been so dumb to risk the baby's life too."

"Is she all right?" Molly asked.

"So far."

"Isn't that good?" Josh sounded confused. "Can't you quit worrying now?"

"The doctor said we'd have to 'wait and see' if she develops normally. It's too early to tell if there's something wrong here—" Karla pointed to her head. "What if what I did caused brain damage?"

There was no way to answer the question. Sarah squeezed Karla's hand more tightly.

Suddenly Josh realized that he'd left the camera running and turned to see Gary manning the post. Quietly and a little shamefacedly, he returned to the camera.

"Sorry," Karla murmured. "I didn't mean to burst out like that. It's just that I don't *want* to go home if the baby's damaged in some way. It will just be more proof of how stupid I am."

"Ridiculous!" The word burst out of Sarah so violently that both Karla and Molly looked at her in amazement.

Sarah blushed but continued. "If that's what happens, you'll need your family more than ever. Maybe you could manage on your own, but you shouldn't have to. Do your parents have any idea what's been going on with you?"

Karla bowed her head. "Not much. We had a terrible fight. I've told my sister everything but made her promise not to tell Mom or Dad."

"Then you'd better tell them," Sarah said firmly. "You and your parents are both hurt and angry. Make the first move toward them—let them help you. Maybe you'll be surprised."

"And if I'm not?" The pain on Karla's face was terrible to see.

"Then you aren't in any worse shape than you are right now, and at least you will have tried."

"But what if they can't forgive me?"

"That's their problem. The only one you can control is *you*, and you can forgive them. It says in Luke 6 '. . . love your enemies . . . expecting nothing in return. Your reward will be great.' I think you'll have to take the first step. Parents are proud and stubborn sometimes because they're human, just like the rest of us. It's worth a try."

A tiny smile graced Karla's lips. "Maybe I will. I

can't make the mess I'm in any worse, can I? Besides, if they do want to see me, then my baby can meet her grandparents, right?"

She looked at Molly's watch. "What time is it?"

"Six-fifteen."

"If I left now, I could catch them both at home." Karla looked pleadingly at Sarah.

"Scram! Interview's over," Sarah said with a smile. "And let us know how things turn out."

Molly dropped into the chair Karla had vacated and gave a noisy sigh of relief. "I feel as though I'm on an emotional roller coaster! Do you think her parents will speak to her?"

"I hope so," Sarah said. "I've never seen a person who needs her parents more. I hope her dad knows about Colossians 3:21."

"I don't know about it," Molly said. "What does it say?"

" 'Fathers, do not provoke your children, or they may lose heart.' "

"You've got a Bible verse for everything, don't you, Sarah?" Molly observed. Her comment was not a jibe but sounded like real admiration.

"I don't, but I do believe that every circumstance we can get ourselves into is addressed somewhere in the Bible. God's pretty thorough, you know."

Molly leaned back in the chair and folded her arms across her chest. "I never thought much about God or praying until I met you, Sarah, but lately, after meeting all these girls my age with so many responsibilities and problems, I've been feeling like I should be doing something for them. Do you think praying would help?"

Sarah's smile was like sunlight breaking through clouds. "Absolutely. There can never be too much prayer."

"I like this!" Chrissie held up a neon sleeper that practically glowed in the fluorescent lights of the department store. "What do you think?"

She turned to Molly, Sarah, and Rochelle Parker, the young woman who was Chrissie's "volunteer" from Haven House. Rochelle was pale and slender. She wore her brown hair in a straight bob, which she kept pushing behind her ears to keep out of her eyes. Her white skirt and pink shirt looked very preppy next to Chrissie's black leggings and oversized man's shirt rolled at the sleeves. "It's . . . bright."

Chrissie's face fell. "You don't like it."

"No, I didn't say that. It's just a color I'll have to get used to," Rochelle said tactfully.

Today's assignment was to buy baby clothes, and Molly and Sarah had asked to tag along.

"There's no way a baby could go to sleep in that color," Molly said bluntly. "How about something not so noisy—like a pastel."

"Boring," Chrissie concluded but dropped the

neon sleeper for something more subdued in mint green. "Hey!" She stared at the price tag. "This one is on sale. I could buy two of these for the price of one of the others."

"Excellent!" Rochelle said, pleased. "That's exactly the right thing to do. Your budget is limited, so it's much wiser to buy economically. Besides, that neon might fade when you wash it."

"I suppose you're right," Chrissie admitted. "I have a lot to learn."

Sarah turned to Rochelle. "Do you have any children?"

"Two. A boy who is five and a little girl who is two."

"Have you volunteered for Haven House long?"

"Chrissie is my third girl." Rochelle smiled pleasantly at the burgundy-haired teenager as she pawed through a stack of reduced-price rompers. "It's been very interesting."

"Interesting?" Sarah echoed. "In what way?"

"My first girl ran away from Haven House shortly after she arrived. Since I'd had the most contact with her, I was helping her parents and the police track her down."

"Did you find her?" Molly asked.

"Actually, she found me. She missed her baby and was weak and tired. After two nights on the streets, she managed to locate my house. She was asleep on my lawn furniture when I woke up in the morning.

The experience taught her that Haven House was an all right place to be."

"What happened to her?" Sarah asked.

"She's going to school part time and works evenings at a fast food place. Her sister is baby-sitting for her. It's not easy, but I think things will work out. I pray that they do."

Chrissie appeared carrying a pair of tiny patent leather shoes. "I've got to have these. Aren't they adorable?"

"How much do they cost?" Rochelle asked gently. "Is it in your budget?"

The look on Chrissie's face told her that it wasn't. "I'll never be able to buy anything!" she wailed. "Not even shoes for my own kid!"

Rochelle took the situation in stride. "Of course you will. Not today, perhaps, but someday." Deftly, she changed the subject. "I'm feeling a little tired. Can I buy you girls something to drink?"

They agreed, but Chrissie insisted she had to go to the ladies' room first. She reappeared about ten minutes later. Sarah, Molly, and Rochelle had saved her a place at the table.

Chrissie's demeanor had changed since the incident with the little shoes. She appeared sullen and unwilling to talk. She wouldn't even bring her eyes up to meet those of the other girls.

They made uncomfortable small talk until their sodas were gone. Then Rochelle turned to Chrissie. "Did we get everything on our list? Lotion, clothes, a new T-shirt for you. . . ." She picked up Chrissie's shopping bag.

"No!" Chrissie reached out to stop her, but it was too late. A tiny pair of shoes tumbled out of the bag. Chrissie grew pale.

Molly and Sarah knew instinctively that Chrissie hadn't paid for those shoes. Rochelle knew too.

She turned to Molly and Sarah. "If you'll excuse us, Chrissie and I have a few things to talk about privately."

Chrissie sank a little, as if she were wishing that the floor would open up and swallow her whole. Sarah quickly rolled away from the table and Molly followed her.

Outside, Molly and Sarah stopped to stare at each other.

"Shoplifting!" Molly finally said. "I knew she wanted those shoes, but . . ."

"I suppose she thought there was no other way she could get them," Sarah said. "Who knows how you or I would feel if we had a child and no way of buying it the pretty little things we wanted for it?"

"You aren't saying you *approve* of what she did, are you?" Molly asked, alarmed.

"No way. And I'm sure Rochelle will do whatever is necessary to straighten Chrissie out. It's just sad, that's all, being a new mother and having so little to offer your child." Sarah's eyes flickered. "When I was a kid, my mom was always making layettes for babies."

"What's that?"

"A little bundle of things a new baby could use—a blanket, a T-shirt, diapers, diaper pins, sometimes soap or powder. Mom collected stuff for dozens of them. Our church sent them to missionaries to give out to new mothers so that their babies could have something of their very own. I suppose that was the only new thing those children had."

Molly sat down on a bench and stared at a squirrel playing in a nearby tree. "Does your mom still do that?"

"Sometimes. Now she makes quilts and gathers school supplies for the boxes the church sends."

"Hmmm," Molly muttered, but said no more.

"Is there any salsa left?" Julie asked, peering over the litter of tortilla chip bags, soda cans, and candy wrappers. "I still have two chips to eat."

"I am so full I could explode," Kate groaned. "Do you guys always chow down like this?"

Julie and Kate had joined Darby, Sarah, and Molly at Darby's house after school to watch some video clips Ms. Wright had recommended. The fact that Julie and Kate had even agreed to come was something of a victory. They usually turned up their noses at such invitations.

"No salsa. Yes, we always eat this much," Darby said. "Does anyone want to finish off this root beer?"

"Are we done with the videos?" Sarah asked. "Or are there more to watch?"

"We're done," Darby said.

"Good, I want to get home and e-mail Steve tonight," Kate said.

"How's the romance progressing?" Sarah asked.

Kate frowned. "It's weird to say, but . . . fast."

"What do you mean?" Darby asked. "How can a relationship progress quickly when you're hundreds of miles apart?"

"I don't know, but it does." Kate picked at an invisible piece of lint on her jeans. "We know each other better than almost anyone else because we don't have anything to share but our thoughts and opinions. We talk about politics, national events, our schools, our parents, clothes, music, everything."

"That sounds good," Sarah commented.

"It is, but I wish he were here. Instead of going rollerblading or to a movie, we sit at computers. Some 'date,' huh?"

"Did you get his picture?" Darby asked.

"Not yet. He keeps promising to send it but he never does."

"Do you think he's hiding something?" Molly asked.

Kate looked worried. "I don't think so. . . ."

Quickly Sarah saw that this conversation might lead to trouble and changed the subject.

"I wish my homework were done," she groaned. "Molly, have you started that English assignment yet . . . Molly?"

They all turned to look at Molly, who was staring absently out the window, a pensive expression on her face.

"Huh? Oh, sorry. I was just thinking about something else." Molly flushed.

"Obviously. You looked as though you were a million miles away. What's up?" Darby asked.

Molly frowned. "I was just thinking about something someone gave me the other day."

"A present? Who was it?" Julie wanted to know.

"Not a present. More like a . . . secret."

"Can you tell us? Or is it a *secret* secret?" Kate's almond-shaped eyes brightened at the thought.

Slowly, Molly stood. She went to her backpack and rummaged through it until she drew out a small floral book secured in a plastic bag.

"A girl came up and handed this to me when I was leaving Haven House. She looked at me for a moment and then turned and almost ran away down the hall. When I opened it, I found a note inside."

"What did it say?" Darby's interest was captured.

"It said that she couldn't be interviewed on television because it would be too big an embarrassment to her family, but that she thought other girls should know her story. So she gave me her diary." Molly lifted the book in her hand.

"That's her for-real diary?" Julie was dumbfounded. "Why would she share that with anyone?"

"Because she thought other girls should know her story," Molly reiterated as if that made everything perfectly clear.

"Well then, what *is* her story?" Kate asked.

"I don't know." Molly stared at the little book. "I haven't read it yet."

"Why not? I would have opened it the minute she ran away!" Julie said.

"I understand," Sarah said. "She gave you something really precious and close to her heart. It's not a book you open just because you are curious. She wanted you to do something with it, didn't she, Molly?"

"I'm sure of it. I've been almost . . . scared . . . to see what it says. Every interview we've done so far has been hard or painful in some way or another. I have a hunch this isn't going to be any easier."

Molly was silent for a moment. Then she looked up and scanned the faces of the girls. "Do you want to read it together? We're all part of the *Live!* crew. The girl meant to share it with us, didn't she? We're the ones doing the show, after all."

"Maybe just you and Sarah should read it," Darby suggested. "You're the ones who have the assignment."

"No, I don't think so," Molly said. "We'd like your input, wouldn't we, Sarah?"

"Definitely. Start reading, Molly."

Molly opened the diary, flipped past a few pages, and began to read about one-third of the way into the book.

> *May 20th*: Prom is tonight! I am so excited I can hardly stand it! Tom says he's got the perfect evening planned, and I just know it's true. I'm getting pink and white roses to go with my dress. He's rented a limousine to take us to dinner and, he says, a really *big* surprise for after the dance! I think he's going to give me his class ring. He

just got it last week and it is so cool. Things are really working out for us. I'm a candidate for prom queen, head cheerleader, and the school newspaper just named us "Cutest Couple" in the gossip column. It's going to be really different next year after Tom graduates. I'm glad he's going to do his first year of college in Brentwood because I couldn't bear to be apart from him. Medical school takes a lot of years, but it's been his dream since he was a little kid. Maybe I'll be a nurse. That way we could always be together.

The girls looked at one another without comment. From the first entry, it sounded as though their mystery girl whom Julie had dubbed "Jane Doe" had everything going in her favor.

Molly turned to the next entry and continued reading.

June 30th: I haven't written for a long time. It seems like years since the day I was excited about prom. The dance was beautiful, all pink and silver with tiny white lights and glittering stars. The band was great and I was named queen. It was the best night of my life. After the dance, Tom didn't want to go to the after-prom party. He said that now was the time for that "big surprise" he'd been planning.

It was a surprise, all right. He'd rented a motel room for us. He said he wanted us to be alone together. I was nervous at first, but after he asked me to go steady and to wear his class ring, well, one thing just led to another. . . .

It's been six weeks since that night, and I think I'm pregnant. What am I going to do? All Tom talks about is college and medical school. I know he'd want to get married if I tell him. Would I be ruining his life? And what about *my* life?

Molly paused and looked up at the girls.

"Wow," Kate breathed. "This is the kind of stuff you've been getting in the interviews?"

Molly nodded. "Heavy duty, huh? Sometimes at night I'm just exhausted."

"You too, Sarah?" Kate asked.

"Let's just say I've cried and prayed more over this story than any other we've done. It's odd, though," she went on, "but these girls really *want* to talk. It's like they've been bottling things up inside and want to get it out. Maybe it's easier to talk to someone their own age too."

"It's easy to talk to *you*," Molly pointed out. "Sarah, you're awesome—so compassionate and understanding. If I were in trouble, I'd talk to you!"

"It's that Christianity thing happening again," Julie commented. "That 'inner glow.' Sometimes I wish I had some of that."

"You can," Sarah said. "It's free for the taking. Christ died for all of us."

Julie wrinkled her nose. "Maybe later."

Sarah burst out laughing. "It's not like shopping for clothes, Julie. The sooner the better. God's waiting for you."

Julie looked around as though He were lurking in a corner ready to pounce. "Read some more of that diary, please?"

July 4th: Guess maybe I shouldn't have picked today to tell my folks, but it was as good as any—and there were definitely fireworks at my house. Mom cried and Dad paced the floor. Then Dad cried and Mom paced. Then we all cried. They want me to go away and have the baby. They say I'm too young to get married.

I told Tom too. I was right. He wanted to run away and get married immediately. Then we started talking about what we'd do if we had a child. I'd have to finish high school or get my GED. He'd put off school to work. It feels like all our dreams are turning to ashes. Our parents are making us go to a counselor. I never meant for prom night to turn out like this!

"Poor girl," Darby murmured. "When you read her words, Molly, I can feel how much she's hurting."

"What happens next?" Kate asked, as if this were a story with a potentially happy ending.

Molly picked up the diary once again.

July 15th: My parents found a place for me to go. It's called Haven House and it's in Brentwood. Our church has something to do with sponsoring it, and the minister told them about it. It's supposed to be a place for girls who keep their babies. It gives them a place to live, lessons and help

> in child care, school classes, and job counseling. It's not exactly the place for me because Tom and I decided it would be best to give up the baby, but my parents don't think I should stay at home. I don't want to go, but I can't stay. I know my parents are paying a tuition for me to be there because we're not in "financial need." I'm scared. I hope Haven House lives up to its name.

"And that's how she got here," Molly concluded. "It looks like the rest of the diary is a day-by-day account of her time since she arrived in Brentwood."

The girls were all silent, lost in their own imaginings of what it might be like to be in the shoes of the mysterious writer of the diary. There was nothing any of them could say.

"He sent it!" Kate barrelled into Chaos Central waving a sheet of paper in her hand. On it was a grainy reproduction of a photo. The boy in the picture looked about seventeen years old. His hair was slightly long at the back and curled at his collar. He appeared to have a pleasant smile.

"So this is the famous Steve, the computer hacker," Andrew said, studying the fax. "He doesn't look so special to me."

"I think he's adorable," Kate said, grabbing the photo from Andrew.

"Did you send him a picture too?" Sarah asked.

"Sort of." Kate blushed.

"Sort of? How can you 'sort of' do that? You either did or you didn't."

"I sent a picture Gary took here in the media room," Kate finally admitted. "Of all of us."

"What's wrong with that?" Darby asked. "We're a great-looking group."

"Some more than others," Andrew muttered under his breath.

"I didn't tell Steve which one was me." Kate's gaze affixed itself to the floor.

"Why not?" Molly asked.

"I thought he'd pick out the girl he assumed was me. I wanted to know if he'd pick an Asian girl. . . ."

"Isn't that sneaky? Why haven't you told him?" Darby asked. "Aren't you proud of your heritage? You should be."

"I don't know. I just wanted him to like me for me—not for how I looked. Now that we've gotten to know each other, it's a little embarrassing to tell him that I kept it from him." Kate looked miserable. "I feel like I lied or something."

"You should tell him right away," Sarah said, "before he responds to the picture. Don't let him embarrass himself either."

"But what if *he* faked his picture too?" Andrew asked. "What if that face belongs to a friend?"

Kate sank into a chair and put her head in her hands. "Dating on the Internet is just as complicated as dating in person!"

"Cheaper, though," Andrew mused. "Hmmm . . . maybe I should try it."

"Ms. Wright, did you have us paged in study hall—oh, hello." Sarah rolled her wheelchair through the door of the media room with Molly close behind. They both stopped short when they saw that Ms. Wright was not alone. Two well-dressed women sat in chairs across from her desk. Both looked exceedingly nervous.

"Girls, I have visitors I thought you might like to meet. Sarah, Molly, this is Mrs. Levinson and Mrs. Winkler."

After polite "hellos," Molly looked beseechingly at the teacher. "What's up?" her eyes said.

"Mrs. Winkler and Mrs. Levinson are on the governing board of Haven House. They came to discuss the project we are doing. They are interested in using some of our materials in a promotional video to introduce people to Haven House and its purpose."

"Cool!" Molly said. "I think it's going to be great once we get all the interviews done."

"Do you need it soon?" Sarah asked, looking concerned. "It's going very slowly. And it's missing something important."

"What is that?" Mrs. Levinson asked.

"I'd like to do an interview or two with the mothers of the girls at Haven House. Parents play such a big part in their daughters' lives—just like the lack of a parent affects a child. I meant to talk to you about this today, Ms. Wright."

Ms. Wright exchanged an odd glance with the two ladies. One of them laughed nervously.

"Great minds think alike," she said.

"What do you mean?" Sarah asked, confused.

"Mrs. Levinson and Mrs. Winkler came here today to 'volunteer their services' to our program. Since the board discussed using our tapes, they've been doing some planning of their own, deciding what other things they might want to add. One of the suggestions was to interview parents."

"Really?" Sarah's eyes grew wide. "So my idea was a good one?"

"Excellent." Ms. Wright laughed.

"We'll have to line up willing parents for the interview," Molly said. "That could take some time and effort."

"You have two right here," Ms. Wright said.

"You both have daughters at Haven House?" Molly asked.

"Not now. But we have had in the past. That's why we are on the board now. Many of the girls who come to Haven House have great financial need. My daughter wanted to be there, and we were able to pay her tuition. She felt she should become independent and yet wanted the help Haven House offered," Mrs. Levinson said. "At the time, there were some problems between us. She felt she needed to be out of the house."

"Why?" Sarah asked softly. "That will be one of the questions that comes up in the interview."

"I was very hostile to the idea of her keeping her baby," Mrs. Levinson admitted. "*Very* hostile. Her pregnancy felt to me like a huge negative reflection on my own parenting. Though I'm ashamed to admit it now, I felt like a failure."

"But it was your daughter's problem!" Molly blurted.

"And, I'm ashamed to say, I made it worse." Mrs. Levinson's eyes looked sad. "I wanted Jenny to hide. To stay inside, to not let the neighbors see her."

"What did your daughter think about that?" Sarah asked.

"Much to my horror, she announced that she wanted to keep her baby. I was dumbfounded at the time. I told her that she didn't know a thing about raising a child—how much it would cost or the wonderful teenage years she'd have to give up. I was sure that Jenny would think the baby was cute for a while, but then become bored with it and that I would be the one who'd end up raising the baby."

Mrs. Levinson wiped a tear from her eye. "I wanted so much more for my daughter than this. I wanted her to have an *easier*, fuller life—college, friends, a career, a happy marriage. When she became pregnant, I believed she put all that in jeopardy."

"So it was *your* dreams, not hers, that were shattered?"

All three adults looked sharply at Sarah. Mrs.

Levinson was the first to speak. "You're a very perceptive young lady. That's exactly what happened. It wasn't until I could quit focusing on myself and start focusing on Jenny that I was able to help her."

"What happened?" Molly prodded.

"Haven House allowed Jenny to learn the skills she needed and continue to go to school at the same time. The baby was in good hands in the child-care facility. Eventually Jenny and I both felt comfortable enough for her to move back home. She's in college now. It's been terribly difficult for all of us, but we're stronger than ever before—and closer too. It took this pain for my daughter and me to really get to know each other and become friends. Our love for each other is stronger than it's ever been."

"So this is a happy ending?" Molly asked.

Mrs. Levinson pondered the question. "Happy? Yes and no. Sex and children are meant to happen after marriage. Jenny agrees with me wholeheartedly about that now. But the mistake was made, and we were forced to deal with it as best we could. Haven House helped. Jenny also started going to church while she was there and invited me to join her. I don't think the real turning point came for us until we began to understand the concept of forgiveness. Sin is sin. But if God can forgive us for our sins, then surely we can forgive others who sin against us. That's what it says in the Lord's Prayer, right? Once I forgave Jenny and she forgave me, God allowed our relationship to blossom."

"And now you're on the governing board of Haven House," Molly concluded with satisfaction. "Cool."

Mrs. Levinson laughed out loud. "God really does work in mysterious ways!"

Sarah turned to the other woman. "Is your story similar, Mrs. Winkler?"

The woman, an attractive, outdoorsy-looking blonde, chuckled. "Just the opposite, in fact. Except, of course, that I too discovered that God could use any situation to work things out. I was the one who wanted my daughter to keep her baby. She was determined to give it up for adoption."

"That's a switch," Molly blurted. She clamped a hand over her mouth. "Sorry."

"No need to apologize. It *is* a turnaround from Mrs. Levinson's story." The blond woman smiled. "I was married when I was very young. My daughter was born only two years after we'd been married. I always wanted another child, but it never happened. After getting over the shock of Missy's pregnancy, I guess that somewhere in my mind I decided that this baby could be *my* second child.

"Missy—like her dad and I—is against abortion, so there was never any argument there. But my daughter thought she was too young to be a mother. I told her I would help her, but Missy sensed that what I meant was that I would raise the baby as my own. Finally, when we were both so frustrated and confused that we had no where to turn, I called Mrs. Barry at Haven House. I thought perhaps she could talk Missy into giving in. Instead, she lined up counseling for both of us. Frankly, it saved the relationship between myself and my daughter. Even though Missy never spent a day at Haven House, we are both grateful for the loving service they offer. It was a very easy decision to join the board when I was asked."

"Every story is different," Sarah murmured. "This certainly isn't a subject that comes in black-and-white, is it?"

"What do you mean?" Ms. Wright asked.

"I know people who think that there is only one right way for things to happen. God planned for us to marry first and then to become intimate, not the other way around. Still, people continue to mix up the order, making shades of gray. If they didn't, Haven House wouldn't be necessary. I'm really glad that the churches understand a place like Haven House—it gives God a great place to work."

Molly scrunched her face into a questioning look. "Can't God work anywhere He wants?"

"Of course," Sarah said. "But think of the two stories we just heard. Nothing happened in the 'right' order, but God, through Haven House, was able to sort it all out for these people. It just shows that even though people sin, we can't give up on them. God certainly doesn't—and when He's involved, miracles do happen."

Ms. Wright gently put a hand on Sarah's arm. "You have the most delightful perspective, my dear. Your presence in my program this year has made even a hardened old teacher and newswoman think about God. Thank you."

Sarah grinned and winked. "Like they say, God's ways are mysterious."

"And," Molly added, "never boring!"

Chaos Central was just that—chaos.

In the middle of the noise and hubbub, Rosie Wright sat serenely at her desk looking over notes someone had handed her. As if attracted to a light in a storm, students started to gather around her. Finally she looked up with an amused smile. "Troubles?" she asked.

"The students in the twenty-first century are too boring," Darby complained as she glanced accusingly around the room. "They are just like us—and we certainly aren't exciting."

"Speak for yourself," Izzy said, brushing a hand through his stubble-like hair. "I think I'm fascinating."

"Point made," Darby sighed. "There's nothing new to report."

"Trade you," Josh offered grimly. "With our story, every time we turn around, something new hits us in the face."

"It can't be that bad," Andrew rejoined. "Can it?"

"It can." Molly pulled up a battered old easy chair and plopped into it. "I feel like I've been on an emotional roller coaster for days. Maybe I've been hanging out with Sarah too much, but I've certainly started to think like her."

"You have?" Sarah asked in surprise. "Funny, I hadn't noticed."

"Sex should definitely be left for marriage," Molly proclaimed. "It causes too many problems beforehand. That 'plan of God' you talk about is a pretty good one."

"Told you so," Sarah said, smiling.

"Sounds like you've been lucky, Josh," Jake said. "Getting to hide behind the camera all this time."

Josh moaned and sank onto the arm of the chair Molly was sitting in. "Luck's over."

"Josh is going to start interviewing the fathers of some of the babies today," Sarah told them.

"That's going to be tough," Jake said.

"Tough is right. There's no way I'd talk to you if I were in that position," Andrew said. "How about you, Shane?"

Shane looked up from his work and shrugged. "Why not? If you've already got a baby, it's not like you can keep it a secret anymore."

"Listen, guys," Josh said eagerly. "I've got a great idea."

"Uh-oh. I hate 'great ideas,' " Andrew said, backing away. "Don't include me in any of them."

"You don't even know what I'm going to say!" Josh protested.

"But I don't like the look in your eyes. You've got something up your sleeve."

"Actually, Gary suggested it. We ran it by Ms. Wright this morning, and she said it was okay."

"It's work then. I knew I was right. 'Great ideas' usually are." Andrew scowled.

"Haven House has a group for teenaged fathers that meets once a week," Josh continued, ignoring Andrew's grousing. "It takes two to make a baby, and the fathers need to accept responsibility and to learn to participate in their children's care. Haven House wants guys to know exactly what it means to the girls to become unwed mothers. They pay a big price while sometimes the guys just go on with their lives—playing football, dating."

"So they sit around and get beat up by someone telling them what jerks they are?" Andrew sneered.

"Not at all. They get child-care training, education, tutoring, and even job training and placement. That way they can support their babies both physically and emotionally. They don't let guys run away from their responsibilities. It straightens out messed-up guys and also gives them a chance to talk to other fathers in the same boat."

"So what does that have to do with us?" Andrew asked suspiciously.

"They are having a meeting tonight at a church in my neighborhood. I want you to come with me."

Shane, Jake, and Andrew stared at Josh as if he were growing a second head on his shoulders. Izzy made a face.

"Us? No way!" Andrew yelped.

"Forget that," Shane added.

"Why do you want us to go along? None of us are fathers!"

"And I don't want anyone to think I might be!" Andrew said.

"Gary thought it would be effective if you guys got into the discussion. They've agreed to allow us to tape the session. I've got a few interview-type questions ready if we need them, but I thought it would be good to do this documentary-style and see where it goes." Josh looked at them pleadingly. "Help me out?"

"No. Uh-uh. No can do." Andrew looked horrified at the thought.

"Are you crazy?" was all Shane said.

Jake and Izzy said nothing.

"Come *on*, you guys! I need you. I don't want to do this alone. I can't! What kind of friends are you, anyway? I'm in desperate need of moral support. You can't abandon me now." Josh sounded panicked. "If I can't count on you, who can I count on?"

"Aw, it might not be so bad," Izzy finally choked.

"It will be terrible!" Andrew retorted.

"I think we should do it," Jake muttered. "Otherwise the guilt trip is going to be merciless. Besides, who knows when we'll need big help with a story?"

"Well, I'm not *saying* anything." Shane, too, weakened.

"You are all nuts! Bonkers! Lunatics!" Andrew stormed.

Ms. Wright cleared her throat. "For the good of the story, Andrew?"

His face fell. He knew he'd been beaten. Once Ms. Wright or Gary got into the act, they always got their way.

Andrew gave a deep sigh. "I'll sit there, but don't expect me to enjoy it!"

"Neat church. Let's look at the stained-glass windows."

"Not now, Andrew. We don't have time. Josh will be furious if we're late. Besides, you don't live far from here. Haven't you been to this church before?" Izzy tugged on Andrew's sleeve.

"Don't think so."

"Sarah and her family go here. I've come a couple of times."

"Izz-man! Sounds serious. . . ."

Before Andrew could turn the conversation in a new direction, Izzy took him by the shoulders and steered him toward the basement, where the meeting was being held.

Gary and Josh were already there, set up and waiting. Several young men sat in a circle. Some visited quietly. Others were silent, busy studying their fingernails. No one was over twenty years old.

"Welcome!" A pleasant-looking man in jeans and a sweat shirt came out of the kitchen area to shake their hands. "I'm Ben Freedman, pastor of this church and leader of the group."

The guys introduced themselves. Andrew mumbled his name so that no one could understand it.

After taking chairs and being introduced—first names only—to the group, Ben Freedman began, first with prayer, then with an explanation of why the group had been organized.

"We're primarily a support group," Freedman said. "Haven House provides many services for these young men. One aspect is a forum in which to talk, air grievances and worries, and to learn from one another. Usually someone has something on his mind. We try to work through things together if we can. Right guys?"

A few heads nodded. It was obvious that the silently rolling camera was casting a pall over the conversation.

Freedman continued. "Usually it's the girl in the relationship that pays the price and is burdened with the majority of responsibility, although I'm happy to say there are young men willing to do their share and to help out."

"Aren't you coming down pretty hard on guys?" a young man with curly black hair and a faint five-o'clock shadow said.

"I don't mean to, Brice, but because the girls physically carry the child till birth, they do have to deal with every single aspect of the pregnancy."

"So how *can* a guy help? It's not like you wouldn't if you could think of something to do." The emotion in Brice's voice made it tremble.

"I can think of ways to help," said a blond guy whose name was Terry. "But my girlfriend's parents won't let me near her. We can't talk on the phone or see each other. I even tried writing a letter, but they sent it back unopened. I want to be with her, to help her, but they won't let me."

He ran shaking fingers through his hair, and it was obvious that he was close to tears. "I know what we did was wrong. We were raised to know and do better. We made a mistake even after we heard all the lectures about saving ourselves for marriage." He looked at the ceiling as if to wash back the moisture in his eyes. "If I could undo anything, it would be to go back and change that night. But I can't. And now everyone treats me like a monster—or, in the case of her family, as if I no longer exist."

He slumped in the chair. "I'm afraid I'm never going to get to see my own baby."

The room was silent as he pulled himself together. Then Terry looked up, straight into the eye of the camera. "I know this is being taped, and I want to say, for anyone out there, listen to your parents and your pastors. Don't get involved in premarital sex. Don't mess up your life by taking things out of order. It's not worth it."

"People sometimes forget the young men involved with this problem," Ben said, more to the *Live!* visitors than to the regular members of the group. "There are lots of feelings to be dealt with and lots of questions to be answered. 'Do we get married?' 'What will my family say?' 'Do I have to quit school and get a job?' 'Can I still go to college and pursue my dreams?' Those are tough questions, and sometimes they have tough answers."

A guy with straight brown hair and dark eyes spoke up. "I'm married," he said, "and I'm eighteen years old. I work nights and go to a junior college during the day. My parents are paying my tuition, but I have to work to support my family. I never realized what it cost for rent, heat and lights, garbage pick-up, insurance, formula, food. . . ." He seemed overwhelmed just listing his responsibilities.

"I study when the baby's not up," he chuckled without humor, "which is rarely. He's got colic and cries most of the time. Sometimes I'd just like to run away. . . ."

"But you won't," Ben put in smoothly, "because you are here, working out your problems, getting a tutor when you need it, learning how to give your wife a break by taking care of the baby. You're doing the right thing."

Ben turned to the visitors. "One of the phrases we use a lot around here is 'When life gives you lemons, make lemonade.' I believe that with effort and prayer and God's help, all these young men can improve their situations. It won't always be easy or fun, but it can happen."

The conversation turned then to child-care, war stories about diapering mishaps, palatable baby food, and naps.

When everyone else had gone, the *Live!* guys sat in the empty circle of chairs and stared at one another. Gary quietly packed up the equipment.

Finally Josh spoke. "Thanks for coming tonight, guys. I really needed you to be here."

"I can see why," Jake said. "Heavy stuff. It really opened my eyes."

"We should play this tape in every classroom at Brentwood," Izzy said. "Required viewing."

"That's not a bad idea," Gary said, taking a chair in the circle. "Let's suggest it to Rosie."

"You mean it?" Izzy was surprised.

"Anything that will get the message across that abstinence is the smartest way to go," Gary said.

"It's weird, isn't it," Andrew mused. "All the hokey stuff Sarah says about the Bible and God's plan actually is right. I used to think Sarah was just talking nonsense, but now . . ."

"Andrew, a Bible thumper?" Shane said in mock amazement. "Can it be?"

"Not yet," Andrew said thoughtfully. "But I have to admit, Sarah's got me thinking."

"They're back!" Chrissie called as Josh, Molly, and Sarah entered the front door of Haven House.

"We've been waiting for you," Tammy said, as if greeting old friends.

Several girls had left their rooms to greet them. One flung her arms around Josh, another touched Sarah's arm.

"We were afraid that you weren't coming. Are you done interviewing?" Chrissie asked.

"Almost," Sarah said. "But even when we finish we'll still visit. We have friends here now."

"It's weird," Molly admitted. "We were nervous when we started coming here. Now since we've been here so much it feels . . . comfortable."

"And now there's someone newer than you," Tammy said. "Two new girls moved in yesterday."

"Really? How do they like it?" Molly asked.

"They're just like we all were when we first came—scared, quiet, watchful. They'll get over it after a while." Tammy's expression was pensive. "You learn to get over a lot of things while you're here."

Sarah frowned at the odd statement but didn't have time to pursue it further. Several girls had surrounded them.

"You promise you'll come back?" a girl known as Lizzy demanded to know. "Come in the evening and watch a movie with us."

"Good idea. Do it Saturday night. None of us have much of a social life anymore. We appreciate getting company."

"We have to wrap up the interviews," Josh said. "Then we'll start to put the piece together. How about if we watch that?"

"I'm a movie star!" Chrissie chirped. She flipped her odd-colored hair away from her face. "Don't I look it?"

Everyone dissolved into giggles and together made their way toward the dining room for sodas.

Shane and Josh entered the weight room at the health club and surveyed the machines.

"So this is where Sarah works out. Impressive," Josh commented. He looked at his own biceps. "I know I could use some work."

"You can come here as my guest three times before you have to join," Shane explained. "See if you like it."

Josh dropped onto a nearby bench and put his head in his hands. "The only muscles I feel like I've been using lately are the ones in my brain—and they're definitely getting overworked."

"How is the story going?" Shane asked.

"It's heavy. Molly and Sarah are doing a great job. They really seem to understand these girls and where they are coming from. Me . . . I'm just listening and learning."

"Come 'ere," Shane said. "I'll show you how to work this machine."

A young blond man was doing lat pulls nearby. He looked up. "Hi, Shane."

"Marc. How are you? Haven't seen you here in a long time," Shane said in greeting.

"Five months," Marc blurted. "The five worst months of my life."

Shane blinked, startled. "What's been going on? Are you okay?"

"Aww, you don't want to hear it. Nobody does." There was a look of despair on the young man's face.

"Try me. You might be surprised. I'm a good listener. And this is Josh. We work together on a student-run television show."

"No kidding? Sounds like you're doing all right, then." Marc's shoulders slumped. "Better than me."

"Why don't you tell us what's wrong. Maybe we can help," Shane offered.

"Help? Nobody can help." Marc's words were bleak and bitter.

"Did you break up with Tori?" Shane asked perceptively.

Marc gave a sharp, humorless laugh. "Break up? Hardly. Or maybe we have. I don't know anymore. Tori's pregnant and her parents won't let me in the door of their house anymore."

Josh gave a sharp intake of breath. Was this story going to follow him everywhere he went?

Shane, sensing what Josh was thinking, just said noncommittally, "Oh?"

"I wanted to get married. I love Tori. Getting pregnant was a big mistake, but I want to take responsibility. It's not like I'd ever run out on her, but her mother won't let her get married. They make her stay home and take care of her little brothers and sisters. She doesn't get to go out. They're so angry that they'll hardly speak to her. Tori deserves better than that, but how can I give it to her? It's like her dad said, I don't have money or a job. What am I going to do?"

Shane whistled through his teeth.

"I don't want the baby to be raised without me. I love little kids. The only thing I do have to give right now is love, and they won't let me do that."

"Then you'd better get busy," Shane said calmly.

"Busy?"

"Sure. Finish school, get a job, show Tori's parents that you can be a good dad."

"It's easy for you to say, Shane. I don't even know where to begin."

Josh cleared his throat. "If you don't mind my interrupting. . . ."

Marc looked up, startled. He had forgotten Josh was there.

"There's a place called Haven House that helps people in situations like yours. It provides a place for unwed mothers to live while they get their diplomas and a job. They have counselors there. Maybe if you and your girlfriend both went, they could help you."

Marc looked interested. "Me too?"

"It can't hurt to ask. It's run by churches. I can't believe they'd turn you away. I can give you the name of the director." Josh scribbled Mrs. Barry's name and number on the back of a deposit slip from his checkbook. "I'll tell her you'll be calling."

Marc stared at the name as if it were a map to hidden treasure. "Thanks. Thanks a lot."

Sarah and Darby met Kate in the hallway. She looked downcast and depressed.

"What's wrong with you?" Darby asked. "Lose your best friend?"

"Sort of," Kate surprised them by saying. "Steve and I had a disagreement last night on e-mail."

"Why? It's not like you had to start a fight. You can think before you speak on e-mail," Darby pointed out.

"I know that *now*," Kate muttered. "It was so silly. He wants to meet me, and I'm not ready. It's just too weird. What if he's a freak? What if he thinks *I'm* one?"

"What about all that stuff about getting to know

each other's minds?" Sarah asked. "Doesn't that count anymore?"

"I don't like blind dates," Kate said stubbornly.

"How's he going to get to Brentwood, anyway?"

"His parents are going on vacation. They're taking a car trip and said they'd come to Brentwood." Kate groaned. "How did I ever get into this mess?"

"Oh, the computer age," Sarah said with a smile. "We have so much to learn!"

"Happy birthday to you. Happy birthday to you. Happy birthday dear . . . *everybody* sing! Happy birthday . . ." Ms. Wright glided through the media room door on sneaker-clad feet carrying a huge birthday cake with enough burning candles to qualify as a three-alarm fire. Scraping and clatter filled the room as the students pushed away from their desks to make room.

"Whose birthday is it?" Julie asked.

"Molly's," Jake said. "Didn't you hear us talking about it earlier?"

"And Gary's," Ms. Wright added, much to her cameraman's embarrassment. His cheeks flushed pink.

"You shouldn't have, Rosie. I quit celebrating birthdays when I hit thirty."

"Nonsense," Ms. Wright said briskly. "Do like I do. I add a year to my age in the even years and subtract one in the odd years. Works great. I haven't aged a bit, and I always get a party. Now, grab a knife and start cutting."

She had thought of everything—plates, napkins, ice cream, forks and spoons, and two party hats—one for each embarrassed birthday person.

After his third piece of cake, Izzy leaned back in his chair and rubbed his stomach. "Mmm, that was good. I love parties. I think this one should continue at my house after school. How about it?"

"Fine with me," Andrew said. "If I go home, I'll have to work at the restaurant or do homework." Andrew's parents owned an exclusive restaurant in Brentwood.

"Me too," Julie and Kate chimed together.

The others were quick to agree.

"Go ahead," Ms. Wright said, "but count me out. I have a class at the Last Chance Ranch tonight."

"How is everyone there?" Izzy asked. He and Shane had done a special story on the juvenile boys' ranch and even spent a little time inside the walls.

"Fine. They always ask about you and Shane," Ms. Wright said with a smile. "They call you the two 'crazies' who *wanted* to spend the night at the Ranch."

Izzy turned to Gary. "How about you? You're the birthday boy. Can you come?"

"I don't know. . . ."

"My sister doesn't work tonight," Jake said slyly. "I'll bet she'd drive me over."

Gary blushed. He and Jake's sister occasionally dated—much to the delight of the *Live!* crew. It was great material for teasing. "Let me call her," he said. "I don't trust any of you."

Jake pretended to be hurt, clutching his heart and falling to the floor. While he was sprawled on the tile, Izzy ate Jake's cake too.

"Can you turn that music up?" Izzy asked. "I can barely hear it."

"That's because the foundation of the house is shaking and windows are starting to crack," Gary growled. He dived for the stereo and protectively shielded the volume control.

"You're showing your age, Gary," Izzy retorted cheerfully. "Go ahead, turn it down. We understand."

"Thank you." Jake's sister uncovered her ears and relaxed against the couch cushions. "Aren't you afraid of damaging your hearing?"

"Not really. I never play music that loud unless there are adults around," Izzy said with an impish twinkle. "What do you think I am? Crazy?"

"Good party, Izz-man," Shane said as he walked by with a slice of pizza in one hand and a can of caffeine-loaded soda in the other.

"Does anyone want to play pin the tail on the donkey?" Molly asked. "I love that game."

"Grow up!" Andrew yelped. "Besides, there's no way I'd put a blindfold on in this crowd. Who knows what you might do to me."

"Pin the tail on the donkey is sounding better all the time," Jake said with a laugh.

Sarah appeared in the doorway with a packed

pizza pan. "More, anyone?"

"I'm stuffed," Josh said.

"Me too," Darby replied. "Besides, I think it's time to open the presents."

Gary and Molly both looked up. "You got us *presents*?"

Darby waved a dismissive hand. "Don't worry. We didn't spend a lot of money. Just a few gag gifts."

"Uh-oh," Gary muttered. "Time to go."

"No way. This is the part I came to see!" Jake's sister, Kathy, said.

"You can open your gift first," Darby said to Gary, handing him a large box wrapped in the obituary page from the newspaper. "Because you're the *oldest*."

"Not that old," Gary protested weakly as he untied the black ribbon from the box. He opened the lid carefully, as if what was inside might go off. A startled expression flitted across his features followed by a smile. "And I'm certainly not *this* old!"

He began to lift items from the box—prune juice, soaking solution for dentures, muscle rubs for sore muscles, a variety of laxatives, reading glasses, a book printed in extra-large type for easy reading, and a sample package of the newest supposed cure for baldness.

"Yes, perfect!" Molly held up a tiny pink bib when her box was opened and Darby had pointed out that this was for someone much *younger* than Gary. "I've been thinking that I should do something for the girls and their babies at Haven House. Now I can bring them a whole box of things to pass out. What a great idea! Oh, I love you all so much!"

Jake and Andrew shrugged. Izzy grinned. "So much for the 'gag' gifts. We wanted to bug you. I guess we're just nicer than we thought!"

Gary popped the cap on the prune juice and passed it around the room, encouraging everyone to have a sip, while Molly admired the tiny gifts in her box.

After a few moments, Sarah cleared her throat. "I have an announcement!"

The room quieted slowly, and all eyes turned toward her. She was smiling broadly. "I have some great news, and I want to share it with my very best friends."

Now she had everyone's complete attention.

"As you know, I work out at a health club several times a week. Izzy, Shane, and Darby have all been there with me. Lots of people are surprised that I choose to do that—until I explain how important it is for me, and all wheelchair-bound people, to maintain upper-body strength. I know it seems weird to see people on crutches, in chairs, and with walkers exercising, but we really do need it.

"I must have made an impression on the management at the club, because yesterday they asked me to lead an exercise class for the wheelchair-bound at the gym!"

"All right! Way to go!" Izzy jumped up and gave Sarah a hug. The others started clapping.

Sarah's face glowed. "This is like a dream come

true for me. I can do something 'normal' people do, and I can make a difference."

Darby put a hand on Sarah's shoulder. "You don't give yourself enough credit. Even before this, you've made a difference in *my* life."

"Darby, guess what!" Sarah's voice was high-pitched and excited as it came over the phone line. "You'll never believe it!"

Darby rubbed her eyes and looked at the clock. It was eight o'clock Saturday morning. "You're right. I don't believe it. Call me back when I'm awake."

"You have to wake up right now. I want you to go to the health club with me."

"Get real, Sarah! It's Saturday morning. Why do you want to go there, anyway? You lift weights all the time as it is."

"I need to warm up. I'm going to be in a race this afternoon!"

That woke Darby. "A . . . race? You?"

Sarah laughed. "That's right. Wheelchair-bound, non-runner, unlikely athlete *me*. Dad registered me in a race for wheelchair athletes. We just found out about it yesterday. Isn't it great?"

"But don't you have to train or something? Can you just sign up and run—er, push?"

"I don't see why not. It's not the Boston Marathon. Besides, I have to start somewhere. Ever since I lost the use of my legs, I've wished that just once I could run and feel free. Here's my chance!"

Darby chuckled. "What you have is a need for speed, Sarah."

Darby was thoughtful as she hung up the phone. If daring to try was what made winners, Sarah was definitely a winner. You could triumph without making a trophy. That was what the story of Haven House was all about—making the best of a bad situation. Not giving up. Daring to continue when all the odds are against you.

"Cool," Darby said aloud as she entered the shower. "I guess I know a whole lot of winners!"

It was early morning, and several of the *Live!* staff had gathered in Chaos Central to do some studying before class. Ms. Wright and Gary were having coffee and visiting quietly. Sarah shattered the companionable silence when she rolled herself into the room crying.

Izzy jumped to his feet and hurried to her. "Sarah? What's wrong?"

Sarah tried to speak, but sobs kept choking back her words. Tears streamed down her cheeks.

Everyone, including Ms. Wright and Gary, was immediately at her side. Darby grabbed a tissue box and handed a wad to Sarah.

When her tears subsided, Izzy maneuvered her chair to the center of the desks and tables. "Can you tell us what's happened now?" he asked gently.

"Oh, Izzy, I feel so sad!" Sarah's sweet mouth trembled.

"Has something happened to someone in your family?"

Sarah looked up. "Oh no, nothing like that!"

"Then why are you so upset?"

Everyone stared at Sarah as she rubbed at her eyes and blew her nose.

"Tammy called me this morning. Do you remember her?" Sarah asked Molly and Josh. "Tammy was the girl we interviewed first. Her baby's name is Aimee."

"She was the one who was so crazy about her baby," Josh said. "She didn't even want to put her down."

"And she even spelled her baby's name in a unique way so it would be more special," Sarah added. "She called to tell me that she's given Aimee up for adoption."

"No way," Molly said. "Not her. She's the least likely of all the girls to make that decision."

"She decided it was just too hard. She couldn't handle the responsibility. Every time her sister or her friends went out and she stayed home, she felt resentful. She didn't want it to be that way, but it was. At first it was fun, but Tammy began to think about everything she was missing—education, travel, fun. But that wasn't what made her decide to give up the baby.

"She'd see families in the park with their children and think about Aimee not having a daddy. She began to realize that Aimee might be better off with two parents rather than one. She started to consider what she could do for a baby and what an older couple might have to offer. The more she thought about it, she realized that Aimee would have a better, easier life with adoptive parents than with a teenager who was still dependent on her own parents."

Sarah wiped the remnants of tears from her eyes. She'd regained her composure and was now telling her story calmly.

"Mrs. Barry sent her to one of Haven House's counselors to talk over her feelings, and the counselor gave her a list of questions to ask herself before she made any decisions about the baby."

"What were they?" Kate asked.

"Tammy was supposed to ask herself what *she* wanted out of life. Was she willing to give up her own freedom? Would she have the energy to handle both a job or school and a baby? Was she willing to spend the next eighteen years more concerned about Aimee than about herself?"

"I'd think that, for Tammy, most of those answers would be 'yes,' " Molly said.

"That's what she said too," Sarah agreed. "But those weren't the questions that really got to her. The counselor asked Tammy if she could deal with 24-hour-a-day responsibility. What would she do if she got upset with the baby? Could she, in spite of being tired or stressed, have complete patience with the baby? Did she know how to make sure the baby is always safe and healthy? Could she get and carry medical insurance? What kind of day-care facilities were available to her? Question after question until Tammy nearly went crazy."

"I'd go crazy too," Julie said. "How can we know all that stuff? We're just kids!"

"Exactly," Sarah said. "And for the first time, Tammy began to think that maybe she was keeping Aimee for the wrong reasons—to look 'grown-up,' to have someone to love her, to keep her from being lonely, to make her happy."

"What's wrong with that?" Andrew asked. "They sound like pretty good reasons to me."

"You don't get any guarantees with babies, Andrew," Sarah said. "You can't make a child love you and take care of you in your old age. That's the selfish idea, not what's good for a child."

"So I'm selfish," Andrew said with a shrug. "Good thing I'm not a father yet."

"And that's what you're trying to get across in this story, isn't it?" Ms. Wright asked. "That becoming a parent too young is a very difficult thing?"

Sarah sighed. "I felt so sorry for both Tammy and Aimee when she called that I couldn't quit crying. But Tammy told me that having a baby wasn't what she expected. She thought it would be wonderful to have a baby so she wouldn't be lonely. What she discovered was that now there were two of them being lonely together."

"I really thought they'd make it," Molly said of Tammy and her baby. "I really did. I was sure Chrissie would be the one giving up her baby if anyone did."

Josh laughed. "I saw Chrissie at the mall the other day. She'd given up growing out her hair and dyed the whole mess burgundy. She was still wearing black. But she was happy. The baby is doing great. Her boyfriend is gone and she's glad. She said she never should have gotten into this mess, but now she's doing the best she can to recover. They're just getting by, she said, but she was sure things would be getting better any day now.

"Chrissie told me that she's started going to church at Haven House and thinks it's pretty awesome."

Josh shook his head. "If determination can get you anywhere, Chrissie will go far."

"There's good news too," Molly added. "Karla's parents want her to come home."

"Hmmm . . ." Julie had her chin propped into her hand and was staring off in the distance.

"What are you thinking about?" Jake asked her.

"My cousin's baby. I remember the day I came here with those photos and said it would be neat to have a baby to raise."

"That's how this whole story got started," Molly reminded her.

"I know. And now I've changed my mind. I'd never want a baby so soon. It was immature of me to think that I might. I guess that plan of Sarah's is right."

"God's plan, not mine," Sarah corrected with a smile. "And He is always right."

"Hurrying home to e-mail Steve?" Molly teased as Kate hurried toward the door. "Why don't you let us walk with you?"

Darby poked Molly in the ribs with her elbow. "Maybe she doesn't want us along."

Kate's step slowed. "No, it's okay. He hasn't been writing as often since I told him he couldn't come to Brentwood to visit me."

"Are you sorry?" Molly asked.

"I don't know. I guess it all happened too fast. I'm used to getting to know guys in person. Meeting someone in cyberspace was just too weird for me. I kept wondering if he were actually an ax-murderer or something. I think I'll stick to guys I know from school."

"So that's it?" Darby asked.

"For now. We agreed to keep writing occasionally and to have other e-mail 'friends,' " Kate said.

"So you might date occasionally but you aren't going steady anymore?" Molly translated.

"Right." Kate sighed. "It's hard not to be jealous, but if I don't want him for myself I guess I can't keep him from talking to other girls."

"One thing is for sure," Darby commented. "Dating in cyberspace isn't any less complicated than dating in person!"

"Oh, I don't know," Molly said. "You don't have to comb your hair or brush your teeth or even get dressed to date in cyberspace. Maybe someday *no one* will meet in person until they decide to get married!"

The room was totally silent as the video ended. Gary got up and pressed the rewind button. "Well, what did you think?"

They had just finished viewing the Haven House story.

"Awesome," Shane whispered. "I had no idea. . . ."

"I don't know how you did it," Izzy said, "but it was terrific—moving, compelling, heartrending. . . ."

"You can quit now," Josh said with an embarrassed laugh. "With your vocabulary you could go on all night."

"You did a fantastic job," Darby concluded.

"Gary and I have to agree," Ms. Wright said. "You three have put together some impressive footage. Good job."

Molly and Sarah blushed. Josh squirmed with pleasure.

"Ah, Ms. Wright," Molly stammered, "I have a question."

"Yes, Molly?"

"Next time you give us an assignment, could it be a little more . . . lighthearted?"

Ms. Wright smiled. "Take you off the emotional roller coaster, you mean?"

"Something like that. Sarah, Josh, and I have agreed that we're *exhausted.*"

"How about a story on the potbelly pig farmer who gives them manicures and little jackets?" Andrew suggested.

"Or the lady who makes artwork out of the dust bunnies underneath her bed?" Jake added.

"There's a guy in my neighborhood who collected matchbooks," Shane offered. "He had thousands, but one day he lit a match and *poof!* no more collection. Now he's collecting the pens and pencils businesses give away as freebies. It's 'safer,' he says."

Each suggestion was slightly crazier than the last until everyone was exhausted from laughing. Then the morning bell rang, and the media room emptied as the students hurried to class. Molly's question was left unanswered. What *would* they cover next for *Live!*? They would have to wait for another day to find out.

Love is in the air at Brentwood High and takes all kinds of forms—from an Internet romance to an infatuation with a handsome young exchange student from Greece. Will the *Live!* crew be able to concentrate on producing its television show if some of its members are more interested in romance than class projects? Find out in book #7 of the exciting LIVE! FROM BRENTWOOD HIGH series.

Turn the page for an exciting
Sneak Preview
of

Pamela

A Judy Baer
SpringSong Book

1

"Yahoo!"

Pamela Warren winced as she glanced at the cigar-chomping reporter next to her in the *Winnipeg Star* press box. He was so ebullient that she had difficulty concentrating on this final period of the Blazers' game. Though not well-versed in the rules of hockey, even she could see that player number 48 had saved the game with his hard-fought final point.

Raising his stick high in the air, the skater, clad in red, white, and blue, gave a victory sign as his teammates ushered him from the ice. Pam tore her eyes from the hero of the moment and spoke to the whooping man next to her.

"He's very good, isn't he?" she ventured.

"Good? Good! Lady, he's the best center the Blazers or any other professional hockey team has ever *had*!" Winnipeg had been giddy all winter over the return of a professional hockey team to their city. "Where have you been all winter to just be noticing that now?"

"In Arizona, actually. Where I grew up. I'm Pamela Warren—the new sportswriter for the *Winnipeg Star*." Pamela extended a slim, finely manicured hand to the paunchy, red-faced fellow.

Grabbing the slender fingers in his beefy ones, he sucked deeply on the unlit cigar and said, "So you've never seen Tiger skate before? Well, you've had a treat tonight! He's never been better!"

"This 'Tiger'—is he Mr. Tyler Evans, the man I have listed on my interview instructions? I was told to interview a Tyler Evans after the game. He's expecting a reporter from the *Star*." Pam studied the chicken-track scrawls of her editor, wondering anew what she was doing at a hockey game on her first night in the city. Her bags were still packed in the trunk of her car while she found herself here, edging with a stocky stranger toward the Blazers' locker room.

"Tyler—Ty—Tiger. Whatever. Tie 'em to their seats Evans—he's one and the same! You'll never find another hockey player like him. We're lucky to have him. Your editor must have a lot of confidence in you. Mine would never waste an interview with Ty Evans on a dame!" With that, her burly partner veered toward the locker room.

Fighting the crowd to follow him, Pam bit off an answer. This assignment had been purely accidental. She would already be in her new apartment by now if the sports reporter assigned to Tyler Evans hadn't called in sick just as Pam had stepped into her editor's office. She had begun to regret reporting her arrival to her new employer. And regret turned to self-reproach as she heard the threads of conversation floating from the locker room.

"Here comes the press! Better put your clothes back on!"

"Nah! Give 'em something to talk about!"

Crude language and laughter, which made Pamela's eyes widen in dismay, emanated from the locker room as she shadowed the hefty man she had met in the press box. Horrified, she realized that there was only one other female reporter muscling her way into the room. But that hard-faced lady seemed oblivious to the bawdy jokes coming from the half-naked men on the benches.

Pam shuttered her eyes in alarm as a bare-chested man in only a towel shot toward the shower room. She could only imagine her parents' horror if they suspected the situation in which she found herself. It was a rude contrast to the sheltered, unsullied existence she had always known.

Prickles crept along her spine as Pamela felt eyes watching her. Glancing around the congested locker room, her gaze fell on the one quiet player in the room. He was utterly composed in the midst of chaos. Aware of her riveting stare, his compelling, golden eyes locked with hers, and much to her chagrin, he began shedding his clothes—slowly, purposefully, daring her with his eyes to turn away.

One glove followed the other to the floor, tumbling across the already discarded helmet. He pulled the shirt over his head, somehow maintaining the magnetic gaze that held Pamela fast. Methodically he undid the laces of his protective padding and let the bulky gear drop to the ground, and Pamela found her eyes resting on a broad, blond-furred chest.

Mortified that she had not looked away, Pamela shook herself from the hypnotic stupor the man had engendered and cast her eyes discreetly to the floor.

Hoping he had forgotten her presence, Pam looked up only to be met once again by catlike eyes. She struggled against them, drowning in the golden, green-flecked orbs.

Suddenly those eyes opened wide in surprise as a bottle of champagne was dumped unceremoniously over the tousled blond head. Pam breathed a sigh of relief as the player turned his back to her to pursue the offender. Grateful for the reprieve, she sought her only acquaintance in the room.

"Well, you got your questions ready?" Her cigar-chewing colleague was at her ear.

"I thought we'd talk about the game," Pam stammered, thankful for a diversion.

"Listen, lady, Ty Evans doesn't grant interviews often. Don't waste your time with that. Go for a scoop. Something about his personal life. From what I hear, he could give you an earful."

"I don't even know which one he is," Pamela complained, glancing over the players, thankful her father didn't know where she was. She was sure he wouldn't approve.

"If you don't know Ty Evans, then why have you been staring at each other ever since you walked into the room? You sure you just moved from Arizona? 'Cause Ty Evans saves *those* looks for women he knows well—really well, if you get my drift."

Stunned, Pamela shrank against the wall. No doubt about it—she had already made a fool of herself in the eyes of the man she had come to interview. Now her mind couldn't formulate a sensible question if her life depended on it. Panicking, she turned heel, poised for flight. She couldn't turn in a story on this man. She couldn't even face him.

"Going somewhere?"

The golden gaze had her trapped again. Droplets of water rained across his shoulders from his showered head, beads collecting in the furry hairs of his chest. Barefoot, he wore only expensive-looking khaki slacks and a leather belt. Pamela found herself staring anew.

"I need to leave. I shouldn't be here."

"Why? You have a press tag. The press are always in here after an important game." He shifted from one bare foot to the other, and the thick muscles of his chest rippled in the fluorescent light.

"I'm only here by accident. It's not my original assignment. Maybe we could talk on the phone. I'm sorry, but I have to leave now." Pam shook her head and backed toward the door.

"Are you from the *Star*? I wondered who was going to do the interview! Wait till I get dressed, and we'll get out of here. Maybe we could get a cup of coffee while we talk. Do you mind?"

Mind? Pamela's brain screamed. She could have hugged him in gratitude. She wanted nothing more than to be away from this raucous, unfamiliar atmosphere.

Outside in the hallway, Pamela leaned against the concrete block wall and willed her trembling legs to be still. Tonight she had already seen and heard more of what her father labeled "the world" than she'd experienced in twenty-two years as a pastor's daughter. The small Christian college she had attended had its share of team sports, but she was convinced that the language in their locker rooms was vastly different from this one.

As she stood with eyes closed, her first sign that she was not alone was the fresh smell of cologne and soap whirling in her nostrils.

"Ready?"

Pam's eyes flew open. Before her stood Tyler Evans, golden boy of the Winnipeg Blazers, wearing a bulky Irish sweater. His hands were jammed deep into the pockets of his slacks, pushing back the front panels of a resplendent calf-length raccoon coat.

Words stuck in her throat as she found herself gaping at

the masculine sight before her. "A . . . but . . . yeah. . . ."

He smiled briefly, apparently accustomed to his effect on women, and replied, "Okay, then. Let's go."

Taking her by the arm, he steered her from the arena by a back passageway used by the players and arena employees.

The bitter chill of the air slapped her back to her senses, and Pam found herself shivering as they stepped into the night.

"Cold tonight, I hear," Ty commented tersely. "Radio said it would get to minus twenty-nine degrees before the night is over."

"Is that Fahrenheit or Celsius?" Pam chattered, not really caring, knowing only that it was far colder than she had ever before experienced.

"Celsius. It's minus twenty or so degrees in Fahrenheit. Are you from the States or something?"

"Uh-hum." Pam shivered. "Arizona to be exact. I didn't know anywhere but the Arctic Circle had weather like this!"

Ty laughed. "This isn't so bad. It's a fairly still night. When the wind blows, *then* it feels cold! Why do you think everyone up here wears fur coats?"

"Well, I've never liked the idea of killing animals for profit and vanity, but"—an icy blast hit them as they came around the corner of the building—"maybe it's not such a bad idea after all!" Her sturdy cloth coat seemed to be made of paper, and the boots that had been ridiculously warm in Arizona felt like plastic slippers on her feet.

"You want to drive your own car or come with me?" Ty had his hand on the door of a little red Porsche and was looking at her inquiringly.

Against her better judgment, knowing she should never

get in a car with a total stranger, Pam chattered, "I'll go with you. My car is several blocks farther down. I'd freeze before I got there."

Ty nodded and ushered her into the soft leather interior. Pamela noticed him working with the front of the vehicle for a moment before he slipped into the driver's seat and flipped the ignition. The car sputtered to life. Momentarily Pam could feel gusts of cold air spurting from the heating system.

"It will warm up in a minute. Where do you want to go?"

Baffled, Pam replied, "Why, I don't know. I've only been in Winnipeg three hours, and most of that time has been at the *Star* and the arena. Where do you want to be interviewed?"

"*Three hours?* You've only been here three hours and you're already working? How did that happen?" Ty took the initiative and pulled from the parking lot.

"I stopped at the newspaper office on my way into town to introduce myself to the editor and tell him I'd arrived. I drove from Arizona and didn't want them to be concerned about me. Just as I got into his office, the sportswriter who was to interview you called in sick. So he gave me the job." Pam huddled over the front heater, which was finally breathing gusts of warm air. "I arrived at the beginning of the third quarter. I had to park about a mile away. It was a very exciting game, though—what I saw of it."

She could feel rather than see Ty shaking his head. "And where do you plan to stay tonight? On your new desk with a computer keyboard for a pillow?"

"The paper rented me an apartment. They said it was close to the downtown area, only a couple blocks from Portage Avenue, wherever that is. Are you familiar with it?"

Ty hooted at the question. "Portage Avenue is hard to miss. The early residents of this region carried their boats from one end of what is now Winnipeg to the other, from the Red River to the Assiniboine, hence, Portage Avenue. Now it's one of the main thoroughfares in Winnipeg. You really *are* new, aren't you?"

Pamela was feeling more displaced by the moment.

"Do you mind if I eat while we're talking?" Ty inquired, glancing sideways at his companion for the first time.

"No. Not at all," she assured him, surprised that he would ask.

"I rarely eat before a game. I don't want it to all come up if I get jammed in the stomach. Like crepes?"

The man was certainly straightforward, she decided. Maybe an interview wouldn't be so difficult after all. "Sure, but it's your decision. I stopped and had a sandwich about four o'clock."

"Well, it's nearly eleven. I think you could manage to join me. We'll go to a place that has an after-theater menu. They all serve dinners until one or two A.M." He pulled into a parking lot across from a massive gray building with one dimly lit door.

Pam's eyes darted to the right and to the left. The street seemed empty and threatening. Suddenly her parents' warnings began coming back to her, and when Ty ushered her through the door, she breathed a sigh of relief. They were inside a cozy cave of a room with sloping walls and dark, discreet tables nestled underneath.

The hostess greeted them. "Good evening, Mr. Evans. Good game. May I take your coats?" Pam's eyebrows raised in the dim light. She was obviously in the company of a Canadian celebrity.

"Can you give us a quiet table near the back?" Ty requested. For a moment Pam was flattered, but then she remembered that she was here to work. Sharing a cozy table with Tiger Evans would be a one-time experience.

While following him down the long corridor of tables, Pam studied his light, athletic walk. He was power and muscle from head to toe. Ty pulled out a chair for her, leaving Pam to face the dining room. He took the chair that left his back to the crowd.

Instinctively Pam realized that he didn't care to be recognized. Adoring fans could ruin a meal—or an interview—rather quickly.

Service was instantaneous when one was dining with a celebrity, Pam discovered. An effusive waiter hovered nearby, and Ty had only to lift a finger for the man to be at his side, eager to serve.

"What do you want to eat, Miss . . ."

"Warren, Pamela Warren. I have to apologize, Mr. Evans. I don't know what you think of me, coming here with you like this. I suppose it's very unprofessional, but my head is still swimming with the newness of it all. You're being very kind."

Ty chuckled. "I do so few interviews that this could be standard procedure for all I know. I surprised myself by agreeing to this one. Got caught at a weak moment, I suppose."

He shuffled restlessly in the chair, obviously uncomfortable talking about himself. Pam studied him discreetly through the dark fringe of her lashes. She noticed a faint scar running from cheekbone to jaw across his right cheek. It gave him a rough, rakish air that was both attractive and repugnant. The men she had known had not lived life in the manner of Ty Evans. The bawdy locker room still clamored in her memory and the daring manner in which he had removed his clothes, more amused than concerned that she was watching.

"What would you like?" Ty broke into her thoughts.

Pam blushed as she glanced up, hoping those golden eyes couldn't read her mind. "Hot tea would be nice. I'm chilled to the bone."

"No food? I hate to eat alone." He smiled openly for the first time, showing an even expanse of white teeth and a deep rugged slash that could barely be called a dimple in each cheek.

Pamela melted. "Whatever you recommend would be fine with me." Perhaps food would undo the heady feeling she was experiencing.

"Earl Grey for the lady and coffee for me. With extra cream," Ty began. "And two bowls of French onion soup, two loaves of French bread, and crepes suzette for dessert."

Pam's eyes widened. Ty's idea of a simple meal was vastly different from hers. She fumbled in her purse for a notebook and pen, but before she had it opened, Ty began an interrogation of his own.

"So, then. How does it happen that you came from Arizona to Winnipeg—and in December, of all months?"

Pam smiled. "I have a degree in journalism and a special interest in sports writing. Once I graduated, I decided I wanted to see the world. I've lived a rather cloistered existence. It was time to get away. A friend heard of this position, and I applied. More amazing yet, I got it. And here I am." She spread her hands wide, a bemused expression crossing her heart-shaped face.

"And is hockey your specialty?" Ty stirred his coffee, tapped the spoon on the rim, and laid it on the table, intently watching her all the while.

Laughing nervously, Pam shook her head. "No. The closest I've come to a hockey game is in the books I've read. But"—she hastened to assure him—"I'm a very good writer and a fastidious researcher. I'll do your story justice!"

Amusement flickered across his features as he leaned back in the chair. "I'm sure you will, Miss Warren. I'm sure you will. Now what do you want to know about me?" Somehow he had managed to make the casual question seem personal and intimate. Pam found herself blushing like a schoolgirl.

The cigar-chewing reporter of earlier that evening came unexpectedly to her mind. His advice rang loudly in her ears: *Go for a scoop. Something about his personal life . . . he has lots of stories to tell.*

For the first time since they had been seated, Pam glanced around the room. Quickly she discovered that most eyes were on their table, and the fevered buzzing of conversation no doubt included her and Ty Evans. The women especially seemed interested in the broad back and dark gold head exposed to their vantage point. A knot grew in Pamela's stomach. How could she ask a man like Ty Evans about his personal life? And if he were willing to tell her, would she really want to know?

"Well, aren't you going to ask me anything?"

"Uh, well, since I'm so new, maybe you'd better tell me a little about your background," she stammered.

His golden eyes darkened to the color of maple syrup. "What I want the public to know of my background is already public record, Miss Warren. Why don't you ask me something original?"

Pam bit her inner lip. Perhaps she deserved the cut. Where was the courage that had made her the *Arizona Tri-*

bune's most feisty investigative reporter?

"You'll have to forgive me, Mr. Evans, but your fame didn't reach as far south as Arizona. You'll have to give me some information, whether you like it or not."

"Touché!" Ty grinned. "I needed that. Reporters make me nervous. They're sort of like doctors, prying at your innards with pens instead of scalpels, but cutting you up, nevertheless."

Immediately more sympathetic, Pamela began her work, trying to slice from Ty's mind the information that would constitute a "scoop" for her new employer.

A frustrating quarter hour later, Pamela knew no more about Tyler Evans than she had at the beginning of their conversation. He thwarted her every stinging question, answering blandly, revealing nothing.

Finally Pamela became irritated. Forgetting all her father's admonishments toward civility and gentilesse, Pamela blurted, "From what you've told me tonight, Mr. Evans, I can deduce that you are as exciting as a piece of milk toast and as opinionated as a sponge. Come on, *Tiger*, you have a rough and tumble, masculine image to uphold! There's got to be more to you than this!"

"Rough and tumble, huh? Masculine, they say? So that's my image. Well, well. And I've disappointed you? So sorry. Do you want me to see what I can do about that—Miss Priss?"

A startled tremor slithered through her as Pam realized that Ty had put his words into action and slid his hand across the table to grasp her own.

She immediately regretted her abrasive words and pulled her hand onto her lap. She was sorry for her abruptness when Ty raised an eyebrow and studied her thoughtfully. He was to be under scrutiny, not she.

Just then the soup arrived, and Pam breathed a sigh of relief. Ty Evans kept her off guard, just as he did opponents on the ice. She was glad for the respite.

Bowing her head to give thanks for the food, she could feel golden eyes boring into the top of her sun-blond hair. She raised her eyes to meet his and found them filled with gentle amusement. Inexplicably she felt the need to defend her prayerful actions.

"Excuse me, but I always say grace before meals. I—"

"You don't have to make any excuses to me, Miss Warren. I don't make any for my actions. You shouldn't have to either. I believe your habits are purer than mine." Ty shifted in the chair, stretching his long legs until they grazed Pam's.

"But I thought—"

"Act on what you believe. Don't apologize for it. I never do. I respect people who stand up for what they believe. Don't move to Winnipeg and change that about yourself, Miss Priss. I think that's what I'm going to like best about you." Ty smiled that genuine, unguarded smile again and nearly took Pam's breath away.

She reached shakily for her notebook and jotted the words "animal magnetism" onto the page. Whatever she wrote about Tiger Evans, that phrase would have to be included. There was no other way to explain the charm he exuded. Whatever the "scoop" turned out to be, it would no doubt stem from that magnetism.

Aloud, Pam responded, "Thank you for that. I'm glad to know you believe as I do—"

"Oh, I didn't say *that*! Don't get me wrong. Just don't

compromise yourself here in the big city. That's all." Ty chuckled, obviously amused that she had thought him to be a believer.

A finger of disappointment marched down her spine. She was already wishing desperately for a Christian friend in this unfamiliar place. Then the cold light of reason came back to her. How dare she think of Ty Evans as a friend? How presumptuous and unreasonable! He had consented to do an interview with another reporter and gotten her instead. She had begun to mistake politeness for friendliness. And for a moment he had made her forget how alone she was in the city that was to be her new home. Sadly she turned to her meal. Perhaps food and some sleep would settle her rocketing emotions.

They finished the meal in silence: Ty, lost in thoughts of his own; Pam, wondering how she'd make a story of the infinitesimal scraps of information Ty had given her. She wouldn't make a very good showing her first time out.

"Well, ready to go?" Ty's voice broke into her weary thoughts. The day had been a long one.

"Yes, please. The meal was wonderful, but I'm getting very drowsy. I left Sioux Falls, South Dakota, at seven A.M., and now it's after midnight."

"No wonder you look like you're about to cave in. Come on. I'll drive you back to your car."

Pam stopped at the till on her way past, but the waitress said, "Oh, madam, Mr. Evans took care of your meal. Everything is paid for."

She caught up with him in the front entry, shrugging into the lustrous fur coat that made him look like a giant bear. "Mr. Evans, I meant to pay for our meal. This was my interview, remember?"

Ty chuckled. "If I don't like the article, I'll bill you. Come on, now, bundle up. They say the temperature has been dropping steadily since we got here."

Pam shuddered as they stepped from the warm café. The wind had increased, and an icy blast whirled around her legs and through her cotton pants. Ty seemed oblivious to the tempest and sauntered toward the Porsche. He held the door for her, and she scurried inside away from the arctic howlings.

"Have you quit shivering yet?" Ty asked as they neared the arena parking lot. Her car was the only one left in the lot, now empty and quiet.

"I'm afraid I'll never get used to this." Pam's teeth chattered so much that the words were nearly unintelligible.

"Sure you will. And this year you'll see a white Christmas. It's worth a little cold."

"I don't know," Pam muttered, her face buried in the front of her coat. Her body was trembling with a violent force. "I'm so cold I'm not sure I can get my key in the ignition."

"Well, I'll wait here until you get the car started. Can you find your way to the apartment?"

"I have the address, and now I know where Portage Avenue is. I should be able to find it. Thank you, Mr. Evans. It was very nice to meet you." Pam shimmied from the car and ran toward her own. Once inside, she fit the key into the ignition and turned it to the right, waiting for the comforting growl of the engine springing to life.

Nothing. Tears came to her eyes, and the two that fell to her cheeks hung there in frosty dismay.

"Troubles?" Ty was at the window, his big fur coat buttoned high under his chin against the wind.

"It won't start."

"We should have moved it to my parking space and plugged it in."

"Plugged it in to what?"

"Plugged in the block heater. So it would start. You *do* have a block heater, don't you?"

"I'm not sure. What does it look like?"

Ty glanced at the car's front grid. "No block heater. Well, I'll give your car a jump. Stay where you are."

Pam shivered in the cold vehicle as Ty pulled his car up to face hers. Pulling cables out of the trunk, he lifted the hood of her car, obscuring the view.

"Now try it," she heard him yell. Shortly her own car sprung to life and he slammed the hood into place. As he returned to her window, she could see frost on his eyebrows and the tips of his hair.

"Thank you. How did you do that?"

He grinned like a frosty polar bear. "Tomorrow you get this jalopy to a garage and have them install a block heater. And from now on, whenever you park the car for more than a few hours, plug it in. There will be outlets in all the parking places at your office and apartment building. This isn't Arizona. And another thing," he continued before Pam could get a word in, "get some warmer clothes. Buy a snowmobile suit or sleeping bag to put in the trunk of your car. If you ever had trouble in that flimsy stuff you're wearing you'd be a Popsicle before anyone found you. Now give me that address, and I'll show you where you live. I wouldn't sleep tonight if I left you in the parking lot to find your own way home."

Not waiting for Pam's gratitude, he trudged to his own car and pulled into the street. She followed, thankful that she didn't have to make one more decision on her own. If she'd become lost tonight, she would have wept in dismay. Independence was beginning to seem more charming in theory than in actual practice.

Shortly the Porsche pulled in front of a tall building with large wooden doors. Ty jumped out and came to her window. "You've got indoor parking here. Follow me up the ramp. Since your apartment is on the tenth floor, I'll park on ten if there's a space." He disappeared into his car, and the car pulled away again, turning into the serpentine ramp.

By the time they were parked, Pamela's legs were shaking so she could hardly stand. Nervousness and exhaustion were finally taking their toll. Ty took the keys from her shaking fingers and opened the trunk, pulling the top cases from its interior.

"Is there anything else in this car that you can't get along without tonight?" He looked like a furry beast of burden under all the cases he'd managed to balance.

"No. That's most everything. It's supposed to be a furnished apartment."

"Okay. Let's go then."

Her key unlocked the security door, and they stepped into the hot, dry air of the hallway.

"Your apartment must be this way." Ty led her to the door and she edged the key into the lock. The door swung open and she stepped inside.

"Welcome home, Miss Warren." His voice was very close to her ear, and it was all Pam could do to keep from jumping. The tiny apartment stood before her, simple but inviting. It was better than she had expected after the harrowing day she had been through.

"Not bad. Small, but it will do the trick. Hope you didn't

bring a lot of clothes." Ty was peering into the single closet.

Pam laughed weakly. "I don't own many, and most of those are totally inappropriate for the weather. I'm afraid I don't even have anything suitable to wear to shop for new ones!"

"You're only a couple blocks from stores interconnected by indoor ramps. Make it that far and you'll be all right. Just go out the north door and turn left. Cross the street and there you are. Are you going to be okay tonight?" Ty Evans turned and studied the shaking girl before him.

"Yes. Thanks to you. How can I show you my appreciation for all you've done?"

"Be kind in the article." Ty winked and strolled toward the door. "I'd better be going. We have a game tomorrow night, and I need some sleep. Welcome to Winnipeg, Miss Warren." With that he gave a wink of one golden, catlike eye and closed the door.

Pam sunk to the floor in exhaustion, finally releasing the emotions she had been so carefully hiding. Tears of loneliness dripped forlornly down her cheeks, and she uttered a prayer to the Father she had been talking to all the way from Arizona. *Oh, Lord, what have I gotten myself into now?*

A Note From Judy

I'm glad you're reading LIVE! FROM BRENTWOOD HIGH! I hope I've given you something to think about as well as a story to entertain you. If you feel you have any of the problems that Darby and her friends experience, I encourage you to talk with your parents, a pastor, or a trusted adult friend. There are many people who care about you!

I love to hear from my readers, so if you'd like to receive my newsletter and a bookmark, please send a self-addressed, stamped envelope to:

Judy Baer
Bethany House Publishers
11300 Hampshire Avenue South
Minneapolis, MN 55438

Be sure to watch for my *Dear Judy . . .* books at your local bookstore. These books are full of questions that you, my readers, have asked in your letters, along with my response. Just about every topic is covered—from dating and romance to friendships and parents. Hope to hear from you soon!

Dear Judy, What's It Like at Your House?
Dear Judy, Did You Ever Like a Boy (who didn't like you?)

Cedar River Daydreams

1 ▪ New Girl in Town
2 ▪ Trouble with a Capital "T"
3 ▪ Jennifer's Secret
4 ▪ Journey to Nowhere
5 ▪ Broken Promises
6 ▪ The Intruder
7 ▪ Silent Tears No More
8 ▪ Fill My Empty Heart
9 ▪ Yesterday's Dream
10 ▪ Tomorrow's Promise
11 ▪ Something Old, Something New
12 ▪ Vanishing Star
13 ▪ No Turning Back
14 ▪ Second Chance
15 ▪ Lost and Found
16 ▪ Unheard Voices
17 ▪ Lonely Girl
18 ▪ More Than Friends
19 ▪ Never Too Late
20 ▪ The Discovery
21 ▪ A Special Kind of Love
22 ▪ Three's a Crowd
23 ▪ Silent Thief
24 ▪ The Suspect

Other Books by Judy Baer

- Adrienne
- Dear Judy, What's It Like at Your House?
- Dear Judy, Did You Ever Like a Boy (who didn't like you?)
- Paige
- Pamela

9607

Teen Series From Bethany House Publishers

Early Teen Fiction (11–14)

HIGH HURDLES by Lauraine Snelling
Show jumper DJ Randall strives to defy the odds and achieve her dream of winning Olympic Gold.

SUMMERHILL SECRETS by Beverly Lewis
Fun-loving Merry Hanson encounters mystery and excitement in Pennsylvania's Amish country.

THE TIME NAVIGATORS by Gilbert Morris
Travel back in time with Danny and Dixie as they explore unforgettable moments in history.

Young Adult Fiction (12 and up)

CEDAR RIVER DAYDREAMS by Judy Baer
Experience the challenges and excitement of high school life with Lexi Leighton and her friends—over one million books sold!

GOLDEN FILLY SERIES by Lauraine Snelling
Readers are in for an exhilarating ride as Tricia Evanston races to become the first female jockey to win the sought-after Triple Crown.

JENNIE MCGRADY MYSTERIES by Patricia Rushford
A contemporary Nancy Drew, Jennie McGrady's sleuthing talents promise to keep readers on the edge of their seats.

LIVE! FROM BRENTWOOD HIGH by Judy Baer
When eight teenagers invade the newsroom, the result is an action-packed teen-run news show exploring the love, laughter, and tears of high school life.

THE SPECTRUM CHRONICLES by Thomas Locke
Adventure and romance await readers in this fantasy series set in another place and time.

SPRINGSONG BOOKS by various authors
Compelling love stories and contemporary themes promise to capture the hearts of readers.

WHITE DOVE ROMANCES by Yvonne Lehman
Romance, suspense, and fast-paced action for teens committed to finding pure love.

9606